What

Life is beg... ...ar Island! You are invited to attend as Alice McIntyre is about to take that step as her family and friends attend her wedding to Seth.

Meanwhile, Alice's son Tucker has poured himself into the ranch after losing the love of his life several years ago. He's watched his mother start over after losing his dad, and he's watched his brothers find love and happiness. But can he? And then Maggie walks in and sets his world spinning.

Lisa has found satisfaction being the chef at Star Gazer Inn and is so happy for her friend Alice's newfound love. After her own horrible divorce, she was determined not to ever even date again, but she is having a hard time denying her attraction to her assistant chef, Zane.

Once again, relax on the Texas coast and enjoy your stay as Alice, her sons, and her friends continue to find love on the South Texas coast with its sparkling topaz water.

You'll want to dip your toes in and stay awhile.

WHAT A HEART'S DESIRE IS MADE OF

Star Gazer Inn of Corpus Christi Bay, Book Four

DEBRA CLOPTON

What a Heart's Desire is Made of
Copyright © 2021 Debra Clopton Parks

This book is a work of fiction. Names and characters are of the author's imagination or are used fictitiously. Any resemblance to an actual person, living or dead, is entirely coincidental.

All rights reserved. No part of this publication may be reproduced, distributed or transmitted in any form or by any means, including photocopying, recording, or other electronic or mechanical methods, without the prior written permission of the publisher, except in the case of brief quotations embodied in critical reviews and certain other noncommercial uses permitted by copyright law. For permission requests, the author through her website: www.debraclopton.com

CHAPTER ONE

From her apartment window of the Star Gazer Inn, Alice McIntyre stared at the beautiful ocean just beyond the inn's gardens. Her heart was hugely delighted with what this day was going to bring: her wedding to Seth.

The inn was closed for this weekend as it was all about her and Seth, gathering with her family and friends for their wedding vows. She'd never thought she'd be doing this again but was so blessed to have found Seth. She took a deep breath and then, with perfect timing, the door to her room opened and her longtime friend Lisa stepped inside.

"Oh, you look so happy." Lisa closed the door behind her.

Alice headed toward her. "Thank you for all you are doing." She embraced Lisa, her friend but also her partner in the inn's restaurant. She couldn't have this wonderful inn without the amazing restaurant. Lisa was a brilliant chef.

Lisa pulled back, holding her shoulders with both hands. "I am thrilled to be able to direct everyone in the kitchen, with producing your food and wedding cake for this wonderful occasion. And no worries after you and Seth leave for your honeymoon. I promise you that the restaurant will be perfect, especially with the help of Zane—that man is amazing in the kitchen. You have trained all of your Star Gazer Inn ladies to do a great job, so they will. Your only concern this week should be you and Seth having the time of your lives on your honeymoon."

Everything Lisa had said was true. "Thank you, and we are going to. All I've been able to think about since he was in the hospital last month was how easily I could have missed out on this if I had put it off any longer. I know that my sweet first husband, William, was rooting for me from heaven from day one. You know, Lisa, yes, my life was a bit different than what you went through. William loved me dearly and we had a wonderful life together. Death just stole him from me, but I've learned that we are designed to love again, if we open our hearts. Personally, I never expected God to put another love in my life. I came to this inn looking for something to do where William and I started out, in this inn. Something entertaining, distracting, and something to give my life a startup again. Immediately Seth entered my life." She paused, taking a breath.

"It's been great watching you two fall in love."

"Yes, and fun, too. Look, I know your marriage ended in a terrible way. You were so wronged and betrayed by that ex of yours having another woman on the side for two years, and a baby before you were even aware of his running around at all. He was awful. Thankfully your divorce went through easily and you were set free and ended up here, where I just know you were meant to be. Now, I know you have said all along you will never remarry or date. There was that one evening when that old boyfriend of yours came to town and I thought you were about to start dating again, but I was wrong.

"However, we both know there is someone out there for you and he is close by. I'm staying out of it but I need to say, don't just shut your heart down because of some horrible pain that you were caused. Open your heart and see the new life that could be waiting for you. Okay—you don't have to say okay. I just felt that I had to voice my thoughts. Honestly, if I hadn't opened my heart, the love that I feel and the joy that I feel about my new life wouldn't be here. I would have just shut Seth out the moment I felt anything for him. Now I can't even imagine doing that. So anyway, I love you, Lisa. I'm so thankful you're here with me—"

"And I'm thankful you are here with me. Today is your wedding day, but I will take to heart what you said. But not today. Today I am concentrating on your new beginning. Your new step into your heart's desire. All your kids are going to be here in a few minutes, and I'm going to stay back and take care of things while they all gather happily around you. They all loved their dad so much, but they love you, and they know how good Seth is to you and how his love had helped put that glow back in you that they see.

WHAT A HEART'S DESIRE IS MADE OF

"Anyway, I just had to come in and hug you and tell you not to worry about anything because it's all handled. And later this afternoon, after we all throw flower petals on you newlyweds as you head to the limo waiting to whisk you off on your honeymoon, don't you worry about anything. Just be happy and relaxed, and enjoy the beginning of your new life with Seth. Love you."

Alice felt so much for this friend of hers who hadn't completely turned down her words. That was progress and made her day even more special, and gave her hope for Lisa. But Lisa was right; today was her day and Seth's day, and that was what she was going to concentrate on from here on out. "Thank you. I love you too."

They hugged again, and then she watched Lisa leave. She turned back to the beautiful view of the inn's garden and the wedding chairs that she could see on the beach from her position. Soon she would walk out there into the sand and the ocean breeze beside the blue water, and her new life would begin with Seth.

CHAPTER TWO

"It looks great, everyone." Nina McIntyre stared at the chairs on the sand just outside the low stone fence that separated Alice's Star Gazer Inn's flower gardens from the sandy beach and beautiful blue water of the bay. They had all discussed where the best place for the ceremony to take place would be. Alice had held a few weddings so far, and had several on the schedule over the summer and into the fall. Most were small and had been held in the beautiful gazebo that Seth had built in the side area of the inn. But one had been held here on the sand, enabling a bigger guest list. There was plenty of room in the gardens and patio for a large reception; it was just hard to have a large ceremony.

WHAT A HEART'S DESIRE IS MADE OF

The sand area was Alice's first choice. Everyone had to think about it but then realized she was right; it would be beautiful. Also, Alice had an entirely different reason than seating. This spot was in the center of where her romance and love had developed for Seth. They'd fallen in love while he worked at the inn and when he took her riding in his boat along the coast, often pausing on the horizon with the inn in sight. These facts made it the perfect spot, with views of both the inn and the ocean.

The chairs had beautiful large ribbons tied to them and the temporary metal gazebo had the same ribbons woven over it, and flowers too. It was gorgeous.

"This is going to make for amazing photos, don't you think?" Lorna, who was married to Dallas, walked up to stand beside her.

Dallas was Nina's brother-in-law and she was crazy about his wife. "Yes, it is."

Lorna smiled at her then looked out to the ocean. "I love it. This area is where Dallas found me crumbled to the ground in labor, and he rescued me. It always means something extra special to me out here."

Nina placed her palm on Lorna's arm. "We are so thankful he heard you and was able to get to you, then carry you to the inn and then to the hospital. What a love story you two have."

"Yes, it was a miracle meant to be. I feel the same about everyone in this family's love story…but especially Seth and Alice. It's going to be beautiful, and they are going to have a wonderful life together."

"I believe so too as does Jackson. He's thrilled. You know, after losing their dad so tragically, it was hard for them. I'm sure Dallas has said the same thing. But watching their mother try to find her new footing was hard. Then she did it—just stepped out there, reached for it, and in the process, God put Seth right there. I love it. This is a wonderful day."

Sophie and Riley walked up, hand in hand, from where they had been rolling out the matching blue rug down the center of the aisle between the chairs. They were not married yet but would be soon. They had put off their date for now because they wanted this to be all about Alice.

"This is just going to be beautiful," Sophie said

enthusiastically. "We may have to have the same thing."

Riley smiled, then leaned in and kissed her cheek. "I'm on board for whatever you want, sweetheart. Just as long as you take my love and walk down that aisle to me."

Sophie's eyes were bright. "I'm so glad I found this family. Alice is such a wonderful woman. I'm so very excited to be here."

"And we are glad you are here," Nina agreed and meant it with her whole heart. "You two have a great energy and just fit. We all thought so from the very beginning."

And they had. Nina and Jackson had talked about it, and so had she and Alice, then she and Lorna. Everyone had been in agreement.

"Now all we have to get married off after Mom and Seth, and then me and this sweet, beautiful Sophie is Tucker. As his brother and knowing all he went through, so similar to the pain Mom went through losing Dad, I'm really hoping his life changes soon, that love finds him again."

Nina hoped so, too, as she and all the girls looked

at him and thoughtfully nodded. Tucker was the last of the four brothers left to find true love. When he'd been in the military years ago, he'd fallen in love with Darla, then lost her to a bomb right before he was sent home. Just the idea was heartbreaking.

She held up her hands. "Okay, I'm going to go up there to the front and tell Jackson and Dallas they have done a great job making sure us gals didn't unhinge the little tent where the vows will be said. They've helped as much as y'all have to get this place set up, now we have to go eat, then get ready since the wedding is a little more than three hours away. We have to be ready for all those coming to cheer them on while we do too. So head that way and I'll bring them in."

They all agreed and headed toward the inn. Nina hurried toward the front where Dallas, Tucker, and Jackson were double-checking the tie-downs after the girls had installed the ribbons and the flowers. They had all stepped back and were examining their work.

"Looks great, guys. Are y'all ready to head to lunch and then get ready? That was a great idea your mom had to keep the inn empty so we would all have a place to stay and dress in last night, spend some time together today, and now tonight have the wedding."

"It was fun." Tucker smiled, then looked back at the canopy. "It looks good. I've enjoyed hanging out with everyone and seeing Mom so happy. I'm going to walk on the beach for a moment, then grab something to eat. See y'all soon."

Nina smiled at him as he turned and headed down the sandy beach alone.

"It has been fun," Dallas said. "I'm going to jog ahead and catch up to Lorna so we can check on the baby…though he's not really a baby anymore since he picked up walking and is a busy little fella. The waitresses have been great, watching him for us. See y'all in a bit."

They watched as he jogged off and called Lorna's name. She turned, smiled, and waited for him. He took her into a hug and then, arm in arm, they walked through the gate into the inn's gardens.

"They really make a great couple." Jackson took her into his arms. "But so do we. You've been wonderful helping this get situated for Mom and Seth.

One of the many reasons I love you."

She smiled at him, her heart thundering as it always did when they looked at each other. "I think so too. And," she said softly as she took his hand and slid it to her stomach, "this baby growing in here is going to be just as happy as their little baby when it comes out and has you as its daddy."

"Ohhh, and you as a mom. I'm excited about when you'll start showing. I don't even feel a bump on your stomach."

"We've only known a month that we're having a baby, so thankfully I'm not showing yet. But honestly, I can't wait either. I'm just so excited…about everything. This has just been such a wonderful year—well, a little over a year since we met."

Jackson kissed her cheek. "Not much more. But it has been wonderful. All right, let's go. We don't want to have to be rushing to get ready and I am hungry. I'm glad they fixed us a buffet in between what they are fixing for the wedding dinner."

She leaned her head against his shoulder as they walked toward the inn. Oh, how she loved this man.

WHAT A HEART'S DESIRE IS MADE OF

This family. Her life had changed so much since his mother opened the inn next to where she was living. That house was now where Lisa lived, the wonderful friend of Alice and chef at the inn. Maybe as it worked out to bring her and Jackson close, it would do the same for Lisa and her new second-in-command chef, Zane. She hoped so. Nina squeezed Jackson's arm. "This is going to be a wonderful day."

Jackson kissed the top of her head. "Yes, it is."

CHAPTER THREE

Tucker came out of the room he'd slept in at the inn last night. He dressed in tan pants, his white, square-bottomed shirt with short sleeves, and his tan loafers that his mother had gotten for all of the men in the wedding to wear because it was a beachside wedding. It was comfortable but not his normal jeans, boots, and T-shirt or Western shirt that he usually wore. Honestly, it had been a long time since he had been dressed like a beach boy. But it was fine because he was happy about his mom getting married, and he really liked Seth. It was mostly a family wedding, with a few close friends. When his mother had decided to marry Seth, she had decided to have the wedding in two weeks, thus another reason it was mostly family.

The setting out on the sand was beautiful and the blue carpet running up between the chairs was pretty. The blue carpet that he would escort his mother up when the time came. He had been stunned when she'd asked him to walk her up the aisle when she had three other sons to choose from. But she'd said it was because he didn't have a mate to stand with beside her and Seth, and therefore she chose him to walk her to Seth in the place of her father, who had long ago passed away. Because of what she'd said about his brothers and their wives—and fiancée for Riley—he was more than happy to escort her. But as odd as it was, he felt a bit sad that he was the only one without a partner in the family.

He went to the front sitting area where the men had decided to gather before the service began, and he walked into the room. They all had the same outfit on that he did; even Seth wore the same thing as they did. Seth looked a bit nervous, so Tucker said hi to all his brothers but went straight to his mother's soon-to-be husband.

"Hey, Seth, how are you holding up?"

Seth let out a breath. "I'm good. I'm ready, but I feel a bit nervous. I'm hoping your mom feels completely sure I'm right for her."

"She loved Dad so much—don't look alarmed, you know she did, just like you loved your first wife. But when she met you, it was the right timing, and you were the right man. Her heart had begun to heal but I didn't think she would ever remarry. That's how I felt, but it didn't take all of us long to know that God had other plans for her. He gave her this beautiful place—well, she bought it but He kept it available until she was ready to see it again and want to revive it. And that led her straight to you. Seth, she loves you, and you've been very good to her."

"Thank you." Seth looked relieved.

"You know I was in love and going to marry the nurse who worked in the camp when I was in the Marines. But she was killed in a bombing right before I came home. All these years later, I haven't recovered from Darla's loss in my life. I've forced myself to date but never felt anything other than friendship and enjoyed the female company. So I can tell you, watching you and Mom fall in love even though you've both lost someone you loved, like I did, has made me think that maybe I'll try to just wait and see when the door to love might be opened again for me. Watching you two has shown me that it doesn't happen until that door swings open, which you two obviously experienced. So don't be nervous. Be excited, because she is going to be eager to reach you as I walk her down the aisle."

"Thank you. You knew exactly what I needed to hear. Believe me, I'm so sorry you lost the love of your life so soon. But I feel confident that you'll meet the new love of your life when the time is right. And thank you for escorting your mom to me. Walk real fast, okay?"

Tucker laughed at that, which he was sure Seth had said to lift the spirit of the conversation. He reached out and hugged him. "If you get the music guy to up the beat of the song, I'll walk her to you faster."

Seth smiled. "Yeah, I'm in a hurry. But I want it to be what your mom wants, so I'll keep my mouth shut and wait."

"Sounds good. See you soon." Tucker turned and instead of walking over to talk to his brothers, he walked from the room and headed to the back patio that overlooked the gardens and then the ocean. He would meet his mom here soon, but right now, his mind rolled with thoughts of Darla. She'd been a wonderful person. A strong nurse. He'd loved her, admired her, and longed for her to be back in his life. She'd been the only woman he'd ever felt those kinds of strong feelings for. Losing her had been devastating. He hadn't yet gotten over losing her and it had been many years.

He took a deep breath and looked out at where his mother was going to get married. He knew his dad would have wanted his mother to find happiness again though he and his brothers hadn't been sure she would. Then Seth had entered the picture, and everything had changed for the better. Now, for the first time since losing Darla, Tucker felt like maybe it was time for him to really start looking because everyone in his family had found love and he had become jealous.

* * *

The wedding was beautiful. Lisa sat at the back of the small group of chairs at the ceremony. She wore a pretty light-peach dress that she'd bought just for the wedding because Alice had asked her to attend the wedding as her friend, not her co-worker. So she had agreed and knew that her crew was doing a great job while she sat here as the true friend to Alice that she was. Alice was the same for her—they'd both helped each other make it through sad times. She now sat in the back row, thoroughly enjoying watching Alice walk down the aisle on the arm of her son Tucker as he walked her toward where everyone else in the family waited for her. Her other three sons and their special women: Jackson and Nina, Dallas and Lorna, and Riley and Sophie, who just got engaged. Finally, there stood Seth, soon to be

Alice's husband.

Lisa was so thrilled for her sweet friend, who had horribly lost her husband a few years ago in a river accident. But she had survived so well, even though she'd grieved deeply. Now, she'd found Seth and her family stood around her, supporting her and looking so happy that she'd found such another true love. One who made her just as happy as their father had made her. It was beautiful.

It made Lisa feel happy watching them, knowing that after you've had devastation in your life, you could start over. She was thrilled for Alice and Seth, who had also lost his beloved wife. But, Lisa wasn't in that position. She hadn't lost the love of her life—or what she'd thought was the love of her life, she had totally and completely been betrayed by the man. Totally startled by the appalling news of his long affair…now was not the time for these thoughts. She pushed them out of her mind and slammed the door. This was not her ridiculous story. This right now was a beautiful, touching scene playing out before her. All the family was smiling as Seth and Alice took each other's hands and their gazes locked while the preacher began.

It was a lovely, simple set of wedding vows said as their glowing eyes held each other and emotion filled their voices. When the preacher declared them husband and wife, their smiles beamed on their faces, and then their kiss sent Lisa's heart rocking. They were going to have a beautiful life together, and she was so glad to be here helping with the coming celebrations.

The preacher introduced them as husband and wife, and they were about to walk down the aisle toward where the celebration would proceed. She stood then hurried through the gate while everyone's attention was focused on the bride and groom.

Zane had supervised everything while she was enjoying the wedding. He, too, was friends with the couple but had insisted that he would make sure everything was done as she wanted while she attended the service. She was so grateful. She had confidence in her restaurant staff, but it was nice to have Zane overseeing and making sure everything was ready for the wedding party.

Zane stood on the top step of the patio that

overlooked the tables that were set up around the beautiful wedding gazebo that Seth had built. Zane smiled as she reached the steps.

"They are coming, and it looks great," she said as she hurried up the steps. Her heels caused her to wobble—he reached out and grabbed her arm to steady her. His touch sent hot waves rolling through her. She tried hard to ignore her reaction to him—something she'd been trying to ignore for a long time.

"Hold on there," Zane said. "We don't need you falling down the stairs and hurting yourself. You look beautiful, I might add. I see them coming, and they look really happy. I think that's wonderful."

She pulled her eyes away from him and saw Seth escorting a joyously happy Alice through the gate into the gardens. "They do look so happy. This is wonderful." She glanced up at Zane and found him looking at her. His warm gaze looked into her eyes, and she couldn't look away.

"I'm really happy for them being able to start over like that. You know, after tragedy strikes, starting over is a really good thing. Tragedy doesn't have to just be the horrible loss of a loved one. It can be your world being ripped apart because someone in the marriage is a traitor."

She swallowed hard. He was speaking directly to her, and he had never really spoken so openly to her like that. "I think we better concentrate on the new couple. So, I'll go check out the cake. Thank y'all so much for the great job y'all did." She pulled her arm out of his and hurried back down the steps, stopping to watch as Seth and Alice paused under a flowered archway in the center of the garden, and he slipped his arms around her and kissed her again.

It was beautiful and hopeful, and to Lisa's surprise, it sent a hard, deep longing raging through her.

* * *

Maggie Carson pulled her car to a halt in front of the small cabin on the McIntyre Ranch. Her friend Nina had recently married one of the brothers who owned the gigantic ranch and asked her to come down. It was a rustic cabin sitting on a gorgeous ranch, in vast ranchland not too far away from Corpus Christi Bay.

There were interesting places all about that she could set scenes or just use the ranch environment. Right now, she felt like it would be easier to just keep it mostly on the ranch but some days she would explore. One place was Corpus Christi Bay, but one place she'd been reading about across the bay was Star Gazer Island. It was pretty in the pictures she'd seen and quaint, very appealing to her. She was much more a small-town girl than a big-city girl, so that was one place she would go often, she thought. But right now, she was going inside the cabin to check it out.

She got out of her car and looked around at the green grass that had been mowed around the cabin and also at the other slightly larger cabin down the gravel road. The two cabins were surrounded by pasture but had fences around the small yards of the cabins and grills to drive over into the small yards that kept the cattle out of the yard. In the distance, she could see black cattle grazing near a pond. She had passed the entrance to the ranch earlier, but Nina McIntyre had told her the entrance to these cabins was two miles down the road, so here she stood.

She would call Nina tomorrow and tell her she'd made it to the cabin. This was Saturday night, and Nina had told her that her mother-in-law was getting married over the weekend and they would all be in town at the Star Gazer Inn until sometime Sunday. However, Nina had assured her that she was welcome to arrive any day she wanted to because the key was waiting for her under the mat.

And that was what Maggie was doing. She walked to the front door mat and pulled the key out from underneath it. She stood back up but before she slipped the key in the door, she glanced down the road at the other cabin. Nina had said the brother's name was Tucker, and that he was quiet and very nice and at night, when he was there, if she needed anything, to ask him.

That was what she'd told Nina—that she needed to be alone and write this new book and hopefully move forward in doing so. She knew that all the McIntyres were very wealthy with the cattle and the oil rigs, so she didn't really understand his living in such a cute but small place.

She slipped the key into the deadlock and opened the door. The living room was wonderful. It was not a normal pieced-together cabin for camping. No, this was a very fancy cabin with a dark leather couch and two soft, rust-toned cushioned chairs on either side facing the fireplace. She could imagine in the winter that the tones went beautifully with a flaming fire in that fireplace. The end tables were light-toned wood and fit in perfectly with the room and furniture. Very welcoming. The kitchen and dining area drew her through the living area to take in its beauty.

A very shiny wooden table that would seat four had a large window behind it that overlooked the pastures. She would be doing a lot of work right there. She turned to study the kitchen, with its light-beige cabinets and granite counters. The lightness of the cabinets, set against the other darker wood walls, along with the large dining area window, gave the wood-walled cabin a brighter look. She loved it and would be able to work here at that table or on that couch or chairs. It was perfect.

She could disappear here for the time she needed.

It was nothing like her and Mark's place in the Plano area outside of Dallas, where she'd known Nina. But she didn't mind it was rustic. Mark would have loved everything about this place. She pushed thoughts of him from her head. She was here to try to move forward…to start back to writing, and to get her life on a new path. It had been two years of not being involved in life anymore. Of just doing what she had to do to get by. But the mourning had taken over, pulling her down into deep, dark shadows.

And finally she'd woken up one morning different, probably being pushed by Mark that it was time. Her mind had gone instantly to writing and he urged her forward, taking the love they had shared and pushing her to start a new life. Then Nina had called—it had been wonderful to hear from her friend and they'd talked, and she'd invited her to come spend time at the ranch in a cabin and maybe start her writing again.

The timing had been perfect and she knew it was time to come to the countryside to write and heal. So here she was, and she could feel her sweet husband's smile at the step forward that she'd taken.

Maybe she could help someone else who had suffered the loss of their loved one. Or help someone find hope again or love after tragedy. Hope was the key word. She personally could not imagine falling in love again. But she was a very good writer and loved making her vast group of readers feel love and happiness as they read her stories.

The thought of doing that again, as she used to do before her husband's death, suddenly rushed through her with an urgency. She could feel the pleasure surging through her that she used to get when she wrote a romance with a happy ending. She was so glad to be here.

Moving outside, she unloaded her car and carried in her suitcases, her computer, her small printer and paper. Her stomach growled, and she knew it was time to find a place to eat and then head to the grocery store. It was time to settle in and make herself open back up to life…a new life. It might take a while, but she'd made the first move and she felt strongly that it was the right move.

CHAPTER FOUR

Tucker pulled into the drive; well, it was really a dirt road, but he had gotten into the habit of calling it his driveway to his cabin. There was another cabin, but it was just a guest cabin, and no one would be in it while he lived in the one right down the road. It was bigger and put him out here in what he'd been calling his place ever since he moved out of the main house. He was eventually going to build a home here on the property he and his brothers owned. He would build, if or when he ever fell in love again and started over. The if was a big word that hung in the air. But if he did, then she would deserve to help him pick out the perfect place to build their home.

This ranch had a lot of land to choose from to build a beautiful house on. But it was the finding a new love that was the greatest hurdle…he was just uncertain since losing Darla.

The first cabin came into view and there was a small car parked in the driveway. Startled, he slowed the truck. The trunk was opened and there were bags of groceries in the back. What was going on? No one had told him that someone would be moving into the cabin—which was strange. Especially because he was just about fifty feet away on the other side of the road. The ranch had a lot of other cabins, and his brothers knew he didn't want anyone visiting in that house while he was across the street. He was going to have to call his older brother Jackson and find out what was going on. He pulled in behind the car, knowing he needed to check this out. When he stepped to the ground and closed his door, he heard someone yelling. *Or was she screaming?*

He instantly jogged up the steps and looked inside the open door. "Hello. What's going on?"

"Help, I'm in the kitchen. There's a sn…snake in here with me."

A snake? He hurried through the living room and past the small wall that blocked this part of the house from the front door view. He halted when he saw a beautiful woman standing on the counter. A stunning lady…a trembling lady. He ripped his gaze off her and looked at the floor and the snake. A very long snake. Relief washed over him seeing what kind it was.

He looked back at the scared woman. "It's a chicken snake, so you're safe. It's not going to hurt you. They are just big and like to scare people while hunting eggs. So just hang on and I'll get it out of here."

"What do you mean, chicken snake?"

"They aren't poisonous. They eat eggs and rats, and he won't bother you."

"I'll just stay up here while you get him."

"Good. Be right back." He hurried to his truck, looked into the pickup bed, and spotted his tire jack. He grabbed it and hurried back into the house. He reached down with the jack and slipped the curved part underneath the snake, then lifted it up.

She screamed and slammed back into the closed cabinets.

"Hang on and let me get rid of him." He hurried to the back door, then across the porch and steps, then across the small yard, where he tossed the snake out into the pasture. That done, he headed back inside to check on the woman.

She had not moved. "Is it gone?"

"Yes. It's okay to get down now." He held his hand out to her, and she studied it. Then, with a big intake of breath, she slipped her hand into his and carefully stooped down, then sat on the counter with her legs swinging over the side.

Her gaze lingered on his. "Thank you. I don't know how it got in and now I'm not sure if there will be more creeping around while I'm trying to sleep."

"I'm Tucker McIntyre. My family owns this ranch, and I live in the other cabin past this one. Do you mind telling me who you are?"

"I'm renting the cabin. Nina set me up. She didn't tell you?"

He had a funny feeling about this. His sister-in-law had set this up and for some reason had not told him. She knew how many vacant guest cabins they had and that he preferred no one be put in this one while he lived in the other one. Something was up. Or there was a mix-up. Whatever it was, it wasn't this lady's fault.

"And your name is?"

"Oh, sorry, it's Maggie Carson. I'm a writer and I came to study the area and the ranch, and write a new book."

"A book." Her words taking him by surprise. "What do you write?"

She looked away and then looked at the floor and hopped off the counter. "Romance with heartache, tension, and new love."

Her words were soft at the end but despite that, they rammed him as if she'd socked him in the gut. "You write romance?"

She stared at him, startled by his question.

He was startled, too. He should have kept his mouth shut. *What had Nina been thinking? Had she done this on purpose?* He would find out. They'd be home from his mother's inn tomorrow night, from enjoying one more relaxing evening after cleaning up from the wedding. He'd just come home earlier because he needed to be alone and to make sure the ranch was making it all right. He'd told them all to send any calls they might get to him and for them to enjoy a quiet night at the inn with their wives. After all, he was the only one of his family who was single now—even his mom had joined the married class once again. He'd just preferred to come home. Needed to come home because he'd watched all of his three brothers get married or engaged—and now his mom—they were all happy, joyful…and he had lost the love of his life all those years ago, and he was still single…alone.

Finding this beautiful woman here had been completely unexpected. Then to find out she was a romance writer was even more unexpected—and unwanted. He stepped back. "Okay, I guess my sister-in-law has a right to rent or hand out time in any of these cabins that she wants. I just hadn't expected this one to be used when I moved out here. However, since you're already here and unpacked, it will be fine. I work on the ranch all day and sometimes the evening too. I'm over the care of the cattle. Making sure they are healthy to be sold or so they can reproduce for the ranch." *Why am I telling her all this?* "Anyway, I guess Nina is going to lead you around when she gets back?"

"Maybe, but I really don't need any leading around. This isn't the first ranch I've ever been on. I know all the interesting stuff about cattle and ranching, so I just might wander around a little bit. I'm going to look at the areas around here because in a romance series, everything doesn't take place at the characters' homes. So anyway, I'm sorry you did not know that I'd be invading your area, and I promise you I won't be bothering you. Thank you for getting the snake out and I hope there are no more."

"I don't expect there will be more, but I don't know how he got in. It's unusual and hopefully that was it. If you need anything, I'll be over at the other cabin in the evenings."

That said, he tore his gaze from Maggie and headed for the door. He couldn't get out of there soon enough.

* * *

Maggie watched her rescuer…her *neighbor* walk out of

the kitchen. She followed him, her eyes sweeping across the floors, on the lookout for another snake.

Tucker had reached his big black truck when she walked out onto the porch.

"Thank you," she called, feeling as if she owed him more than a mere thanks for getting rid of the snake.

He opened the door and paused to look at her across the driveway. "I'm glad I could help. Have a good night."

She started to ask for his phone number in case she needed him again but clamped an invisible hand over her mouth. She would handle the next thing, if there was one, on her own. She'd been relying on friends since losing Mark, and she was determined to get her life back on track. That meant relying on herself no matter what came her way. The snake had startled her, and she'd messed up. But next time something like this happened, she would be ready. If it was another snake, she just had to set up a plan, get a tool to catch the funky creature with—like Tucker's jack or maybe something longer.

"Are you all right?" he asked when she hadn't answered.

"Yes, sorry. You have a good night too."

He tipped the front of his hat at her then got into his truck, backed out and headed down the road toward his cabin.

She walked to her car and lifted out the two bags that still remained in the trunk. She hurried to the porch and set one sack down, then returned to the trunk and with her free hand, she closed it. Moments later, she had both bags on the kitchen counter as she scanned the floor again before unloading them.

Unable to stop herself, she did the floor scan all evening as she moved around the house, looking everywhere she thought a stinking snake could hide. She found nothing and got ready for bed. She left the light on inside the closet to give a little highlight to the room in case she had to get up for anything during the night. She started toward the bed but paused at the window and pulled the curtain back just a bit to look to the other cabin. It had a light on inside and one coming from the back area, probably the back porch, and she wondered whether he was sitting out there, enjoying the night.

Tucker had been nice and though she could have

been upset that there was a man out here in the pastures so close to her, she wasn't. Seeing the light on over there gave her a sense of security. She was grateful for the feeling.

She climbed into bed, reached for her computer and like she did every night, she began working on the next scene of her story. In her heart, she had a good feeling that this would be a great story.

CHAPTER FIVE

The following day, Maggie got up early and made a cup of coffee—a pot, actually, for the day. She filled her cup up and moved to the table where she'd set up her computer and started working. She'd been getting the idea of her book together and she really liked it. She'd already been inspired on the trip to this beautiful ranch. Truth be told, the cowboy who'd rescued her from the snake had helped inspire her. The book was falling into place as she laid out the ideas and even wrote a couple of pages with the hero and heroine just so she could get to know them. She'd done that last night and had been smiling when she went to bed. It had been a long time since that had happened.

She heard her handsome neighbor drive by about six-thirty the next morning. She had a habit of getting up around six, not one who liked lying in bed after she woke up. There had been a time when she could snuggle with her husband. That was no longer the case, so she just got up so she wouldn't lay there missing him like she did the first months after losing him. Getting up helped but this morning, getting up and writing gave her an excitement she hadn't felt in so, so long. Part of that was due to Tucker rescuing her from the snake and how nice he'd been about it.

She pushed thoughts of her neighbor out of her head and started to type. She was glad he was down there just in case she needed something out here where they were alone. She wasn't used to not being near people because she had lived in neighborhoods all her life. But she had no plans of bugging him because she was here to write and explore. Truth was, she hadn't felt a tingle or a nudge of attraction in any way since her sweetie passed away.

But there was also no denying that she'd felt something yesterday. Something she was trying to ignore. But the voice in her brain after she'd gotten her writing done and tried to lay down and sleep had screamed at her all during the night that she should not ignore Tucker.

But no! She was here on this ranch to work on her book and try to move forward. But that didn't mean with another man.

She had just eaten a peanut butter sandwich, her favorite meal when working on a book. Quick, easy, and it didn't interrupt her thoughts. She'd just finished and was throwing the paper plate in the trash—another thing that helped not interrupt her train of thought when she was working and did not want to wash dishes. She'd just headed back to her computer when the phone rang.

She looked at it so she could decide whether to answer it or ignore it until she finished her work. It was Nina, so she instantly pushed the Accept button. "Nina, how wonderful to hear from you."

"Great to hear from you too. I'm glad I'm here today, especially since I was told you got here yesterday. I'm so excited. Can you come up here and visit for a while? I'd love to see you and show you my house. You might get to meet Jackson, although he headed immediately out to the barn when we got here since we've been gone all weekend for his mom's wonderful wedding. I also heard that you met Tucker. He's a great guy. I put you out there near him because I knew if you needed anything at any time of the night that he would take care of you."

"Thank you. He was here for me yesterday. I'm sure he told you about the snake inside the cabin. Thankfully he got it, and I haven't seen another one since."

"I'm so glad he was there for you. So, can you come over?"

She realized then that she'd never answered Nina's invitation. "Yes, I would love to come see your place and you face-to-face. It's been something like four years. So, I'd love to take a break. Although I have to tell you that ever since I climbed in bed last night and started writing, the words have been flowing. I'm loving it."

"I'm so happy. I just knew this would be a great place for you to come and relax and hopefully heal. It's beautiful, peaceful, and inspiring. It's inspiring for my art. I've always been inspired, but when I came out to this area and then here to the ranch, I've been inspired in so many ways. It just fired me up."

"I saw some photos of your paintings and they were amazing. I noticed that some are different than your usual style but amazing. I can't wait to see your studio and your home. Do I just go out this lane and head back to that main entrance to the ranch?"

"Exactly. And as you come down the lane, you'll see the barns and arenas on one side, and the house and yard on the other side, all joined with a large rock parking area. I can't wait. See you soon."

Maggie sighed as she hung the phone up and her heart raced with excitement. She hurried to the bathroom and smoothed on a little foundation, some blush, and a little mascara like she always did before going out in public. Now she was going to see her friend she hadn't seen in several years. Mark had still been alive when she'd last seen Nina, and also the last time she'd talked to her friend; Nina had just disappeared after that conversation.

It had been scary for Maggie. Nina's email no longer existed, and she didn't know what had happened to her. After a couple of years had passed without contact, she'd begun to fear her friend was dead, that something had happened to her. Her work had also disappeared from her normal places she sold from, as if all that she'd had was now bought but nothing new had been added. She'd just vanished, and then Maggie had lost Mark and her life had changed. Neither Mark or Nina were in it.

But she'd known what happened to the love of her life: he'd been killed in a vehicle pileup on the highway and taken her heart with him…and her focus. So, because she still had the same phone number, when she received the call from Nina telling her that she was okay, Maggie had been thrilled and had to sit down, her legs got so weak with relief. Nina explained what had happened in her life and the miraculous way it had all worked out. Maggie had been relieved and overjoyed for the first time since losing Mark at having something as good as her friend being alive and happy to fill her heart.

WHAT A HEART'S DESIRE IS MADE OF

Nina had been saddened deeply when she learned Mark had been killed in the accident and she hadn't been there to comfort Maggie. She'd immediately invited Maggie to the ranch, understanding how her writing mind worked and that she liked to explore an area before setting a series there. Maggie hadn't taken her up on it at first. But Nina's urging had helped Maggie to think about writing again, and here she was at last, getting back into her work…instead of hiding in her loss.

As she drove up the lane, she came up on the stone two-story home on one side of the white gravel road. Barns and arenas on the other side of the large rock parking area stretched from the gate to the house. She pulled to a halt by the gate leading to the house. She was impressed because this place was great looking. The house was a soft beige stone, surrounded by a stunning yard. As she got out of the car, Nina came hustling out the side door. Nina was as beautiful as ever.

"I'm so excited to see you," Nina called, engulfing Maggie in a hug.

"I feel the same way." Maggie hugged Nina, ecstatic to have her back in her life. "Knowing you are okay, and now married to a wonderful man and expecting a baby—oh Nina, I'm just overjoyed for you."

Nina pulled back, her eyes soft as she stared into Maggie's. "Thank you. It's been a real blessing for me to have ended up on Star Gazer Island and have Jackson's mother open the closed inn beside me and then Jackson coming into my life when I needed him most. Marrying him and moving out here and expecting the baby—though I'm barely showing right now—I'm thrilled. Jackson is wonderful and has an amazing family. The ranch is huge, and after talking with you and thinking about the cabins and the surrounding area, I couldn't get you off my mind."

"So you offered for me to come out and to get my mind working on a novel again."

"Yes, and so I made the second call and am so thrilled you took me up on the offer. Now come on in."

They headed toward the house, their arms linked. Maggie hadn't been this happy in so very long she had to fight off tears…of happiness, not sorrow. "You've started a new, wonderful life, it's obvious in the sound of your voice."

Nina led the way into the house and closed the door behind them. "And I'm praying you can while here on this amazing ranch and surrounding territory."

They entered a huge kitchen. "This is wonderful. Nina, I was so down but hearing from you helped me know that starting over can happen. So I'm going to take one step forward and then another every day I'm here, if possible. Mark would have wanted me to. He'd even wanted me to remarry. I'm not sure I could ever do that, but I will strive to find a new life and happiness. That would make him happy."

"And hopefully you too."

She nodded. "Yes, exactly. I'm just so thrilled for you and inspired."

"Great. I can't wait to introduce you to Jackson and his brothers and their loves, and also his mother and the wonderful man who won her heart after her sad loss. She overcame a broken heart when the time was right, and you can too. When the time is right, in whatever makes you happy—that doesn't mean you'll have to fall in love, but if it's meant to be, I hope you'll open up to it."

"I'm not anywhere close to that. Not sure I could ever let myself fall in love again and risk losing someone else. But I am into figuring out my life and moving forward and thankful that you asked me to come visit."

"I'm thrilled you took me up on it. Now, let me show you around. Then we can go outside, where I have my homemade lemonade that you used to love waiting for us. I'll introduce you to my two dogs who are waiting in their special section of the fenced yard that keeps them away from the work at the barns."

"Wonderful. I can't wait."

Nina led her through the beautiful home, explaining that Jackson's dad and mom had built it and his brothers had insisted that Jackson live here in the house. "He and I both love it. Riley lived in a cabin, and he and his fiancée are looking for where they want to build their home on the ranch. Dallas's wife owned a ranch, and he lives there with her and her son. Tucker is the only single one left and lives in the cabin near you. He's a great guy. You'll be safe out there."

"I'll try not to bother him again." She smiled at

Nina, even though she saw her friend's eyes twinkling as she'd been talking about Tucker. *What did that mean?* Nothing, she hoped.

"If you need anything, please do bother him. He's a great man and I think you two can be friends."

"I'm sure he's a great person, but please, don't try to fix me up. I'm not looking for that."

"I'm sorry if it came out like that. I didn't mean it that way. Now, come on, let's go have a glass of freshly squeezed lemonade and visit the pups and talk about what you're looking for out here and what I can set up if you need it. You know, like an escort to interesting areas that might make great scenes in your book. Believe me, I found great places to use as subjects in my recent paintings. Let's go look at those first. Then have lemonade."

She smiled and laughed as Nina hooked arms with her and led her down the hallway to the huge glass room with a tall ceiling overlooking the yard, where the two dogs sat and watched them from outside. "Everything is amazing."

"Yes, I think so too. I'm so completely satisfied

with my life now, and I hope being out here works its magic on you too."

She smiled again and her heart squeezed with hope.

* * *

Tucker had just come out of his office that was right inside the largest barn's entrance. From the doorway, he had a direct view of the parking area and the main house. He'd stood in the shadows just inside the barn's big opening when his neighbor pulled up and parked at the gate entrance to the house. She climbed out and he stepped deeper into the shadows, not wanting to make himself obvious as she headed through the gate to be greeted by his sister-in-law. He watched them. They were obviously really good friends as Nina engulfed Maggie in a tight hug and Maggie hung on as if for dear life. The emotion between them radiated across the distance.

"They are really good friends." Jackson came out of the supply room next to the office. "Nina told me that Maggie had been through a hard time, losing her husband a couple of years ago. Not that Nina hasn't been through a hard time too, but she overcame it and is doing great now. She really felt drawn to invite Maggie out here as encouragement for her to start her writing career again. To begin looking toward her future again. Nina says she's a great author but hasn't written since her husband's death. She agreed after thinking about it and is ready to try moving forward. She's also setting the book series on the ranch—though it will have a new name."

"So, she lost her husband? She's too young to have had to suffer that loss. I guess she's around thirty but still…"

"Yeah, not too far away from your age, and you've been through a similar loss. Darla wasn't your wife but the love of your life. So sadly, you have that in common. I'm sorry she's out there, if it bothers you. I know you like being the only person out there, but Nina talked to me about this on the way home. Telling me she'd given her friend that cabin near you, even though she knew you didn't want anyone in it while you're living there. I hope that it didn't make you mad when you realized what Nina had done." Jackson pushed his Stetson back off his brow a bit and met his stare with concern in his eyes.

"Truth is, at first, it did bother me. But I haven't said anything this morning, because I'm not sure what to say. When I drove out there yesterday evening and saw the car, I stopped to check out who was in the cabin. When I pulled up, I heard screaming. I rushed inside and found her in the kitchen, standing on the counter and staring down at the huge chicken snake on the floor below her. She looked terrified—was terrified. I told her to stay where she was, and I went back to my truck and grabbed my tire jack. I hurried back inside and she hadn't budged from where she was frozen in place. Thankfully the snake also hadn't moved, so I used the jack to pick the snake up. Then I carried it out the back door and tossed it as far as I could into the pasture. She was relieved…so anyway, I was glad to help out since she was so scared of the snake. Also, I think she was as shocked to see me as I was to see her. When I told her who I was and where I lived, she was okay and followed me outside, when I went back to my truck."

Jackson looked relieved. "I figured you'd be able to handle having her out there. At least I hoped so, after hearing her story."

Tucker hitched a brow. "I haven't been interested in dating lately, because I was dating for the wrong reason—trying to get Darla off my heart, not looking for love. Then I started watching all you guys fall in love and something inside me kept yanking at me. Then watching Mom get married this weekend really struck me hard. All of you have become happy, satisfied people, and that's what I'd hoped for myself when Darla and I fell in love. But it wasn't meant to be."

"And I'm so sorry." Jackson's eyes were heartfelt.

"Me too. So anyway, y'all putting a woman out there next to me didn't change my mind about this. It was watching y'all and then Mom being happy that did. It all got me not just thinking about taking a female out to dinner, but to start thinking about who might be the right woman."

"There is another one out there for you. But to find out who she is, you should talk to them and take them out like you were doing before but with a new mindset. Who knows, you might have turned away the right woman because at that time you didn't have the right outlook and now you do. Look back at those nice ladies you took out for a dinner or two and think about if there is any one of them you might want to ask out again. Or think about it in the future when asking someone to join you for supper. Might even think about kissing someone—I heard rumors that kissing with you was not happening."

He stared at Jackson but held back asking him why he'd been talking to women Tucker had dated and asking whether he'd kissed them. But his thoughts straightened out, thankfully, and he knew that Jackson wouldn't have asked that, so he'd heard someone else telling someone about the experience.

"I know, none of my business, and it was just something I heard. Anyway, Maggie is a nice person, according to Nina, and this loss has been really hard on her. Nina didn't put her out there beside you, trying to push you two together. She put her out there because she was worried about putting her out in a cabin sitting on the ranch by itself. She was just thinking that in the evenings and at night that you would be nearby, and if you hear a scream or pounding on your door that you could help her. You know, if she gets scared by the sound of coyotes howling or something like that. Honest, no pressure is meant to be a part of it. Nina says Maggie isn't interested in dating at all. She just needs to put her mind on moving forward and getting back to her writing. And her new life will come as it's supposed to after that."

"I get it. It's all right. I'd have done the same thing, and I'm glad to be there if she needs anything. Like that snake—I don't know what she'd have done if I hadn't driven up. She seemed almost petrified up there. If the snake had crawled off into one of the bedrooms, she might not ever have gotten off the counter. So, I'm glad I was there. I'm going to take the tractor over there and mow around the fence so that her lower grass helps keep more snakes from crawling into her yard. The ranch mowing team keeps all our yards mowed, but this is the pasture area I'm talking about. The cows haven't gotten it eaten down enough yet."

Jackson smiled at him. "You are a good man, brother. I think that's a great idea. I know your sister-in-law will be grateful to you."

"I love my sis-in-law, and you are a lucky man. I'm

glad to help out and, to be honest, Maggie seems like a really nice person, and I hate that she lost her husband. What happened?"

"He was killed in a terrible car pileup on one of the main busy highways through Plano, where they lived. She'd lived near where Nina had lived and that was how they'd become close friends. Nina said he was a great guy, and they had a wonderful relationship...like mine and hers, she'd said, and then hugged me tightly. So, as you can see, there is a strong bond between them and Nina wants to help her. She put Maggie close to you for her protection, not trying to fix you up, so please don't think that."

Relief sank through him. He believed his brother and was touched by Nina's concern for her friend. "I understand now that I know all of this. I'll watch out for her."

And he would. They'd both lost the loves of their lives and he understood all too closely how her heart hurt.

CHAPTER SIX

On Sunday afternoon, Lisa walked out onto the back porch of the inn, which was now free of any trace of the beautiful wedding and ready for the reopening of the inn and restaurant tomorrow to regular customers and not just the family and friends of the inn's wonderful owner, Alice. Who was now on her honeymoon with Seth on a small, private island in the Bahamas, where they'd be for ten days.

All of Alice's family had spent the night in their private rooms here at the inn the night before the wedding and also last night—all except Tucker. He, being the only single one now, had volunteered to head back home to make sure everything was taken care of and be there if there was any kind of emergency with the animals. They had all enjoyed the evening together after all the wedding attendees had left, and then they'd helped get the decorations back down this morning and readied the inn to reopen tomorrow.

Lisa had walked over early from her house next door and was making sure they would be ready to reopen after three days of being closed for the special event of Alice and Seth saying their vows. Vows that had been very touching.

She sighed as she stared out at the ocean, having sat there and listened, and felt her heart rocking with happiness...and wistfulness that she would take a chance on love once more.

She shook her head and inhaled the ocean air as her thoughts went to where they had no business going...to Zane, her right-hand chef. He had taken her place when she was off so she could relax before coming back to work. He'd been the perfect chef, and she was ever grateful he'd chosen to apply for the job, especially considering he was the main chef at the restaurant he'd been at for years across the bay in Corpus Christi. He'd been a blessing in fulfilling her need at the restaurant, but he'd also stirred her heart. She'd vowed this was not something she would ever let happen again. She had good reason.

Very good reason. After her horrible marriage disaster, she'd sworn never to open her heart up to anyone again. She'd been tempted once after she'd divorced and flown to tour Italy, baking with several chefs. But she'd shut down the thought and flown back to Corpus and ended up here working with her friend Alice who'd opened the Star Gazer Inn. Lisa loved it and was intent on devoting herself to the new restaurant and the wonderful customers who returned regularly to enjoy their menu. Zane and his talent fit in perfectly, but had made her vow to herself to not date or get her heart involved with a man ever again harder and harder every single day.

Her thoughts returned to the beautiful, heart-tugging wedding yesterday of her best friend, who'd suffered the horrible loss of her beloved husband and then, as she'd sought a new beginning by opening this wonderful inn and restaurant, she'd found a new love that she hadn't even been looking for. Lisa thought it was a wonderful love story, and Alice was once again amazingly happy and blessed. Could Lisa even hope for another try at love? Alice had known the love of an amazing man not once but now twice. Lisa had been misled by thinking she was loved like that, then totally betrayed for two years before she'd learned her husband had been cheating on her. Her heart had been broken. Then fury had taken over as the sorrow of the life she'd thought she'd had disappeared. She'd always thought herself a very strong person but deep down, hidden from everyone, she'd been raked over the fire and devastated. She never wanted to know that feeling again. Thus, her decision to never open her heart again.

And then Zane had walked in and applied for her assistant chef opening. Since then, she'd been fighting this powerful draw she felt for him. Not that he'd made any kind of advance on her other than when their gazes met, her heart pounded and she felt he had similar feelings. But he hadn't crossed the line to romance; he'd simply been by her side, making her laugh as they worked together and being there any time she needed him…for work.

And yet, lately, she got the feeling if she crossed the line with him, he would gladly open his arms to her. But would it be briefly or forever? He meant everything to her at the restaurant, and she knew she would not risk letting a personal relationship take over and destroy their wonderful working relationship.

She swallowed the sudden lump in her throat and closed her eyes as the soft breeze from the ocean washed over her. These emotions were just stirred yesterday at Alice and Seth's wedding, and she would get them under control by tomorrow when she and Zane would start back to their normal partnership of keeping the restaurant clients satisfied.

"Lisa, is everything all right?"

Startled, Lisa's eyes shot opened to find none other than Zane on the walkway, coming from the side entrance. He wore a soft-blue T-shirt, black, almost knee-length swimming trunks that were often used by many in the area as summer shorts, and his jogging shoes. He took her breath away as the shirt showed off his broad, muscled shoulders that his chef attire hid, and of course the shorts showed off his muscled calves. He might be fifty, but he was every ounce in shape.

"Yes, I'm fine. Just enjoying this beautiful day. I came over to make sure the cleaning was going well and we'd be ready to reopen tomorrow. How about you? Doing good today?"

He smiled, sending a rush of want through her. "I came by your house and your car was there but you never answered your door, so I figured you were either here or taking a walk on the beach. I tried here first, and here you are."

"Do you need something?" *Why was he looking for her?*

"Actually, yes. Seth told me to use his boat today as I'm in the process of finally buying my own and he told me to consider one like his and to take it out today or any of the days while they are honeymooning. So, I am. I wondered, since we never have time off together unless it's almost nine-thirty or ten at night after we've closed, if you might want to take the ride with me. You did say once that you hadn't been out there in a boat in a long time."

WHAT A HEART'S DESIRE IS MADE OF

She was speechless as she held Zane's penetrating gaze. Everything in her desperate to keep her heart closed off from him battled against her as a fierce desire to say yes overwhelmed her. "Umm," she managed. "I need to make sure we're ready for tomorrow."

"I was here last night, and we were ready when I and all the other workers left. Unless you made a real mess after serving those Danish to the family this morning with coffee and juice. Or did y'all party today and not invite me?"

She laughed. "You're right. There is nothing left to do but take the afternoon off like Alice wanted us all to do." She'd given all of her kitchen help the day off today but she'd prepared wonderful Danish herself so it would be ready for her to heat up this morning. She'd come over early from her home next door and heated the Danish, made coffee, and also placed cold orange juice on the counter. All of Alice's family came downstairs at nine and she was ready for them with food out on the patio.

She'd enjoyed visiting with everyone and by noon, after they'd helped her with the small cleanup of their tables, they'd walked on the beach a bit before heading home. The housekeepers had arrived to clean their rooms and make sure the inn was ready for business as usual tomorrow.

Zane was right: there was nothing for her to do here, and she knew it. Now she was being offered the opportunity for a ride on a boat across the beautiful blue waters she'd been staring at for the last thirty minutes.

"Come on, take a ride with me. It's not like we'll have this opportunity again for a long time—or ever, with our work schedule."

He was absolutely right. "Okay, I'd love to."

Zane's smile was instant. "Fantastic. Everything is ready. We'll ride over to my house where the boat is for the week and load up."

"I need to check the doors and make sure everything is locked up then change into some shorts and a T-shirt."

"Sounds good. My truck is already in your driveway, so I'll walk with you and wait on the patio while you change."

She tried to ignore the joy she felt as he walked

beside her a few minutes later toward her house. She should have told him she didn't want to go but that would have been a flat-out lie. The truth was, no matter how much she wanted to deny it, she wanted to spend the afternoon with Zane.

* * *

Keep cool. Build a relationship that surpasses her being my boss. The thoughts rolled through Zane's mind as he drove across town and then pulled into his drive and into the carport attached to his beach house.

"This is where you live? It's so wonderful," she said, her words nearly a whisper of awe.

He smiled at her. "That's about my same reaction when I first saw it. Come on, let me give you a tour inside if you want. Or we can head out to the back and see the water view and the relaxing back area."

"I'd love to see it, if we have time. I'll probably never be over here again, so the time is right."

"Okay then. But you're invited over anytime you'd like to come over."

"Our schedules interfere with that."

"Right. What was I thinking?" He opened his door and met her at the front of the truck. "We have time. This way to the back porch, and I'll open the door." He hoped to hold down the frustration he felt at her keeping them securely in the working relationship.

"The place is beautiful." She walked along the sidewalk around the house, then stepped up the two steps and onto the deck. "I love this deck and that view. You are closer to the bay than my house."

"One reason I chose this was because it has no beach—just straight-out direct access for a boat. Come on inside and then we'll hop in the boat and take a leisurely ride." He held the door open and she passed by him, leaving him breathing in deeply the soft floral scent of her perfume. He had gotten addicted to it in the kitchen when they worked together. It fit her sweet but strong personality.

"It's wonderful." She gasped as she entered his pale-toned living room and kitchen area. He'd chosen a tan leather couch with the same toned chairs and then highlighted the soft room with beach paintings and bird paintings.

"Thanks. I like it. Just walking into the house helps

sweep away any struggle I might be having from a hard day at work."

Lisa turned toward him. "Do you have a lot of hard days? You've never said anything."

Zane should have not said what he said, and her worried expression told him so. "No, I can handle the work and the people. I meant when it's a really busy day and we barely have time to even look at each other, much less talk about anything but the next order. That restaurant has gotten busy, busy."

"Yes, it has and much of that is because of you. Many people I talk to are coming from the restaurant you used to run in Corpus to have your food again."

"And you know good and well they return to have yours. You are a fabulous chef."

She laughed, because they often went through this same back-and-forth about their talents. "And you are too. We have made a perfect match."

He held her gaze as his wish for their relationship to move past the Star Gazer Inn's restaurant burned bright. "Yes, I believe you're right. Now, ready for that afternoon boat ride?"

"Yes, very much so."

And so was Zane. More than ready.

* * *

Lisa sat in the main seat across from Zane as he maneuvered the boat through the water. It was an amazing day, and the water wasn't too rough. It was an easy, smooth ride, and she was glad she'd come to enjoy it. "It's been a long time since I was out on the ocean for a boat ride. It's a perfect day for a ride."

He cocked his head and smiled at her, sending her pulse jumping. "I thought you would enjoy it. I'm going to buy me a boat at last, probably one very similar to this one."

"So you've lived in the Corpus area for a long time and never owned one either?"

"Nope. I worked too much and didn't want to have to take care of one. So I'd go with friends every once in a while. But now, here on Star Gazer Island, I may work a lot but the town is a lot smaller than Corpus across the bay, and I have the money, so why not buy one? Then when I feel like taking a ride, I can. I can also invite my friends along to enjoy it with me."

She liked his thinking. "You'll enjoy it."

"I hope you will, too, sometimes."

"Thanks. If we have time off together again, I'll hold you to that. Oh, look—a dolphin!" She stood, holding the dashboard window in front of her, and watched the dolphin that had jumped from the water dive back in and then another one copy it. The two played before them, and she and Zane watched, locking eyes of excitement together every once in a while.

"That's a great show. They've kept up with us, as if it was just for us."

She chuckled. "I feel really special," she said as they watched the dolphins finally swim off to find the next boat to entertain.

"You are special."

Her stomach twisted at his gentle words. "Thanks. But so are you." She sat back down and turned her chair to face him. "Why have you never married?"

"Never found the right woman and finally figured out that I probably wouldn't. I worked far too much and on the days I took off, I'd date some. But nothing ever came of any of those—yes, I dated a couple of ladies for several months several years apart, but I was never in love. I believe love is the only reason people should get married. Not boredom of living alone so long, not because you're friends, but only because of love...I've never been in love."

They stared at each other, and Lisa's mouth went dry. He spoke and acted on truth. "You speak the truth. I married my ex-husband because I'd been young and thought I loved him. But after he cheated on me and I left the country trying to run from the truth, I realized I never loved him. I thought being needed was love. He needed me to host his parties and cater to his clients. Oh, there was attraction, but I've since realized the difference."

Zane had slowed the boat while she spoke. Now he halted the boat, reached over, and took her hand from her knee, sending lightning rushing through her. She was in trouble.

He stood and pulled her up, his gaze locked on hers. "You are a woman worth loving. I know you aren't interested in me since I work for you and give you your much-needed time off—which I'm more than happy to do. But Lisa, I can tell you that he, the scum you were married to, was an idiot. You are loyal, wonderful, and lovely, and so much more." He stepped close to her, still holding her gaze. "Can I just hold you for a minute and assure you that it was him, not you, who lost in his stupidity?"

She could barely breathe but nodded, knowing full well this was probably a terrible mistake but unable to stop herself from wanting to be enwrapped in his strong arms. As they came around her and the boat rocked gently beneath her feet, she slowly let the breath she'd been holding escape. His chest was hard, his arms strong and reassuring, and his lips brushing against her hair right above her ear had her catching her breath. She had never in her life felt what Zane brought to her with his words, his touch, and his gentleness. Her heart pounded so loudly in her ears that she almost missed his next words.

"You are going to be a blessing to some man in the future, when you're ready to stop letting the last man mess up your future." His arms tightened, and she lifted her head away from his chest and met his piercing navy gaze. Zane dipped his mouth toward hers then paused and stepped back. "Sorry. Now, let's circle this wonderful island we both call home. I've been wanting to investigate it ever since I took my job with you at the inn."

She fought off the disappointment she felt at him not kissing her, knowing he'd made the right decision and wondering why she hadn't. "Yes, let's do that. Sounds like fun."

But nowhere near as fun as the kiss she'd missed out on.

CHAPTER SEVEN

By Tuesday, Maggie had her outlines working very well and she had tested out the description of the ranch. In doing so, she realized she needed more of the feel of the ranch than she had. She was sitting at the kitchen table with a glass of strawberry ice water that she'd made and her computer was open and her notes beside it.

Then she saw Tucker ride up on a big lawnmower. Well, it was bigger than a regular mower but it wasn't a tractor. He let the blades down and began immediately mowing the grass outside the fence. She paused and watched him. He turned the corner once he'd reached the side and headed down the back fence and she still watched him. *Was he the one who normally mowed the grass?* She watched him reach the end of the far corner, and turn and head up the far fence, out of her sight.

She could have believed he was the mower, but Nina had said it was one of the ranchhands and though he worked on the ranch, she seriously doubted he was called a ranchhand. He was an owner and from what she understood, he headed the care and health of all these money-making cattle that ran on this ranch. No, he was not the regular mower. She heard him drive across the front gate and heard a shift of quietness. She headed toward the living room and looked out the window.

He'd reached the driveway on the front before it crossed the cattle guard keeping cattle out of the cabin's yard and away from her car. Now, as she watched, he turned the mower around and retraced his path the way he'd come, making the mowed grass wider outside the fence. At the corner he turned and again, went out of the sides. That fence was on the side of the cabin's bedroom but soon he'd be turning to mow along the back fence again, so she walked back to the kitchen and watched as he came around the corner once again. She picked up her water and took a sip as she watched him drive by. When he reached the far corner, she realized that surely that was the last strip he was going to mow. She set her glass back down and hurried for the front door. She pulled it open and rushed out on the front porch.

She wanted to thank him, so she hurried down the steps and out to the cattle guard and carefully walked across the bars to the gravel road on the other side. She waved as he turned the corner and started her way, along the last short strip to the cattle guard. He pulled to a halt, turned the loud mower off, and grinned at her.

She grinned back. "What are you doing?"

"Well, I was trying to get out here and do this yesterday but didn't make it. So I came today. I'm mowing what I want the guy who mows the yards to start including in the job. He'll be out in a couple of days, so this will clearly be visible. I want them to see what they will now include in the mowing of this yard. Hopefully it will discourage the snakes from coming into the yard but also help you see them if one is heading into the yard. Are you sitting outside at the table some?"

"So far I haven't. I sit at the kitchen table. I have air

conditioning, no sun shining on me but a great view and that's how I saw you as I sat there working and you appeared in the window."

"So you don't like sunshine?"

"No, I do, but since I found a snake in the house, I didn't want to find a buddy outside. But I really appreciate you doing this. I just might open that kitchen door and venture down the steps to that table and test it out. Maybe." She made a skeptical face and to her surprise, he threw his head back and he laughed hard. It was wonderful and sent sparks shooting through her. He had a fabulous laugh and he looked really good in the process, and she couldn't help but stare in amazement at his transformation. Then suddenly he stopped laughing and his expression turned distant.

"Wow. I haven't laughed that hard in a long, long time. Thank you."

Something in the sound of his voice made her think that there was indeed something important in his statement and the laugh. "I'm glad to help. You have a wonderful laugh. It's not too harsh, or too light to make someone think you're fake laughing to make them feel better. It was real and it fit you."

He nodded and gave a slight smile with closed lips. "So how is your book coming?"

"It's coming along great. Honestly, I'm so startled by finally deciding it was time to try to start writing again. Coming out here, I was immediately influenced by the ranch and the ideas started to flow. But I realized just a few minutes before you showed up on the mower that I haven't actually seen the ranch. Other than from the cabin window, this yard, and over at the main house. So, I'm going to call Nina and ask her to show me around."

Tucker studied her then looked out at the pasture before meeting her gaze again. "I could show you the ranch. Unlike my wonderful sister-in-law, I've lived here my entire life, I've explored as much of this enormous ranch as possible. You just let me know if you want me to take you, what might interest you—then I can take you to what I believe matches your want. If you don't know, then I can take you around until something strikes your creative mind. Once that happens I can tell you anything you need or want to know. My dad made sure we knew all about the ranch. Sadly, he's not with us anymore and all we have left is the beauty of this place and the history that he taught us. So the only thing I'll request you not to ask for is a horse ride through the river. We don't do that anymore, not since he died."

Her heart ached for him. He didn't put a lot of emotion in his words, just put them out there as information. But she could tell he purposely kept his emotion down. She had a feeling that he didn't let his emotions out for viewing; instead, what he'd just said was a fair warning of where he would not go. Yet, he'd made an offer that she suddenly knew she needed. She needed this tour given by a cowboy, a ranch owner. The man who felt as much for the land and the history and could pull her into it as he showed her. Just like she needed to pull her readers into the moments in the book.

Her stomach dropped a bit as she understood the offer. Not that he understood what he was offering but she did, and she would be a fool not to take him up on it. "Thank you. You're right, I need you as my tour guide. It might be more than one."

He smiled, his eyes twinkling. "Believe me, I can

get my men lined up and then I'm a free man to take you on as many tours as you need. I do have freedom with my position as an owner, but I have great men who work for me and they can handle it. So, it's just past noon. Do you want to go this afternoon, just to kind of get the feel? See some places and then think about where you might want to go tomorrow? Or the next day? Or when you want to go—I don't want to interrupt your writing, but I am available to show you around. I'm truly sorry about the loss of your husband. My brother told me what happened."

She looked down, feeling the emotion rush through her. She felt gratitude that Tucker hadn't decided to just ignore saying anything about her loss like some people did but had decided to give her his sympathy. "Thank you. Mark was a wonderful man, and I loved him very, very much and miss every day he isn't here with me. But…I'm here because I can't live the rest of my life sitting around mourning. Mark wouldn't want me to. He would want me to start a new life. Continuing my books, which I love, and he loved the fact that I wrote them."

"It sounds like he was a very blessed man to have

your love like that. I am truly sorry and I understand. I don't talk about it much to anybody and I really don't want to talk about it much, but want you to know how much I understand your feelings. Several years ago when I was in the Marines, I fell in love with one of the nurses. She was wonderful and we set a plan to marry. I was getting out soon and she would follow not long after me. But a few days before I was released and flown home, our area got bombed…she was killed." He paused and her heart ached for him.

"I'm so sorry."

He nodded. "I have really struggled ever since. I came home heartbroken and threw myself back into the ranch. My brothers backed off and let me have my time but even though it's been over seven years and I've begun to finally make some forward steps. Personally, I tried dating a couple of years ago but found out all I wanted was to remember her and wish she was sitting across from me. I halted the dating right after that and have just been working hard and enjoying watching my brothers fall in love this last year. I guess I told you that so you'd know I understand where you are at this stage of your loss."

He completely understood her pain, and she understood his. Looking at his eyes, she could see that after all this time, he still cared for his lost love. He wasn't judging her in any way by insinuating that it was past time to move on. Oh, she'd seen those looks and actually heard those words. She'd stopped being angry because she'd realized most people were just trying to get her to start life again. But she wasn't ready…and had no plans to do so until she was.

She had to clear her throat softly before words would come. "I'm very sorry for your loss. We both know losing the love of our lives is terrible. I'm sorry you understand what I'm going through."

They both remained silent after that because there really wasn't anything else to say. They both knew it.

"Maybe we can wait and start the tour tomorrow," she said after a minute.

"That sounds good. I'll line my men out on what to do for tomorrow and pick you up at whatever time you want. Nine?"

"Nine would be perfect."

***

Tucker loaded the lawnmower onto the trailer behind his truck, which was parked at his place, down from hers. Then he headed for his office at the barn. His mind was stuck on Maggie. She was struggling as much as he had, though he was several years ahead of her and realized he had to move forward if he truly wanted to be happy in this life he'd been blessed with. A life his love, and Maggie's love, had lost far too early.

He arrived at the main ranch and disconnected the trailer from his truck but left the mower on it. Then he headed to the barn to check out one of the cows they were doctoring. It was doing better; the swelling of its hurt leg had gone down and he was moving more easily, which was a good thing.

He was in his office later, having gone over the list of cattle needing certain shots tomorrow by his crew. Mitch, his main guy, came in and they went over the details and he told Mitch he would be showing the ranch to someone so he wouldn't be around.

"Is it that pretty woman I heard some of the guys

talking about? They glimpsed her leaving the big house the other day."

"Yeah, she's a friend of Nina's. She's a writer, and I'm showing her some places she might be able to set some of her scenes."

"Really. What kind of writer is she?"

"Romance, I believe."

Mitch grinned and he slapped his thigh. "Now that's perfect. Maybe she'll wake up something that is obviously asleep inside you. I haven't seen her, but the guys said she was hot."

Tucker frowned, not having meant to unleash any ideas among his men. "Look, don't start all that. I'm just helping her out. All right, make sure all this is taken care of, and I'll check in on Thursday."

"We'll handle it. You do what you've got to do and look, friend, enjoy the day."

He couldn't help it; he smiled at his friend and good worker. "I will."

And he hoped he would but mostly he hoped Maggie would. She still had hurdles to make it over where grief was concerned. At least he thought so. He realized that he still had the lifelong love for Darla but his heart might be ready to see whether there was someone out there he could love in this second stage of his life. *Second stage of life*…that was how he was going to have to look at it: Darla was the love of the first years but maybe there was someone else out there his heart could also love. Like his mom had done, and her new husband Seth also. Both of them had been like him and Maggie, having to start over, but they had found each other.

Was there someone else out there for him?

CHAPTER EIGHT

Maggie was waiting outside for him the next morning with a smile of excitement. At least, that was what it looked like to him. She was a very beautiful woman. Her husband had obviously been a very loved and lucky man. His pulse increased, looking at her. Which was a first in a very long time.

That wasn't good. He might have been thinking about starting to look for love again but clearly Maggie wasn't on the market, and he felt guilty about even the thought passing through his mind. He refused to have any ideas of that sort even tiptoe through his thoughts. He was her tour guide and there to help her if she needed anything. This feeling that had passed through him was probably because they both had a sad history in common and that was all. He was adding too much to the fact that his heartbeat had increased at seeing her smiling. He wanted to help her overcome her broken heart if at all possible because he understood what she was going through. But this moment of confused attraction he'd felt had been simply that—confusion.

He hopped from the truck the moment it came to a halt and he jogged around the front end and opened her door for her. "Good morning. Here you go. Hop right in and we'll get this show on the road. My guys were happy to step in and give us time to do this today. They were very clear that we could do it as many days as we needed. I think they were glad to get rid of me."

Her lips twitched upward. "Are you hard to work for?"

"I don't think so. I mean, I give them a chance to do their work, so I think that makes me a good guy." She laughed and he smiled at the sound and the twinkle in her eyes. Much better than their last meeting, with the sadness they'd shown talking about the loss of her husband and Darla.

"I believe you." She slid into the truck seat, which brought their eye levels even.

"Whatever they are thinking, I'm here to help you."

"And I really appreciate it. I've been waiting for this all night, and I can't wait to see the ranch and look for places to set scenes. Cool places for my readers to escape with the characters and forget anything they need to let go of for the time they've delved into my books."

He smiled, closed the door, then jogged back around to his side and slid in to the seat and propped a hand over the steering wheel. Then he looked at her and met her gaze. "So with your writing, do you like to give your readers histories, adventures…what do you actually write?"

"I write romance but while people are falling in love, they are having adventures. Sometimes it can be something a bit scary that maybe he or she saves the other one from. Sometimes it's quite sympathetic and brings out your emotions and sometimes it's funny and makes them laugh. I like to take a little of all of those and combine them into a story but I don't like the stories to be the same, so the characters and the setup is what makes the story different.

"And in this story, I don't actually know yet what is going on in my hero's and heroine's backstories. But we are going exploring and my mind will be working the whole time. I do believe that one of them will have lost the love of their life. It's just…this is my first book since losing Mark, and I can't not speak to that emotion in me. Putting it in the book might help me get stronger and touch a reader needing the same help to deal with their loss or struggle about different things."

"When you're writing a story has it ever helped you through other hard times?"

"Small hard times. I'd never been through the actual heartbreak of losing the love of my life. So honestly, at this point, I don't know if I can help someone get through that kind of loss since I'm living through it myself. But that part of the story will come. Today we're mainly checking places out and seeing what strikes me and inspires scenes in my head and that will inspire the book. Once inspired then we'll go from there."

Her words rolled over in his mind as he tore his

gaze from hers, put the truck in drive and backed onto the dirt road. He was intrigued. He'd thought when a writer came up with an idea, they just wrote it. He'd never thought about how surroundings could help inspire scenes in a book and thus, inspiring scenes could determine the plot or what the book was about. This was interesting—she was interesting. "I'm really glad to be able to help you with this. I'm really believing that your husband would be rooting you on also."

She looked at him and bit her lip. Her eyes had a deep mixture of both sorrow and excitement in them. "I believe he would be. In all honesty, I feel like he is pushing me forward. Rooting me on as you said."

It hit him in that moment that he and her husband had something in common.

* * *

Maggie stared at the beautiful stream that ran through this portion of the ranch. She had told Tucker to bring her to his favorite place. He'd smiled, but if she was right about the look she saw in his eyes, there was a moment of hesitation, and she wondered why.

Now, they had driven a good way across the pastures, toward trees she had finally been able to see in the distance. Trees that ran in a long line across the back of the land. When they'd reached the trees, he'd turned right, off the road, and driven beside the trees a distance and then stopped. Then he'd led her down a trail that wound through the thick trees. She could hear the gurgle of the water before they reached it. The trees grew high over the stream that he'd told her ran from the river not too far away. But he liked this spot and this was where he'd come to think.

Now she turned toward him. "This is so lovely. So how did you find this? It's out here surrounded by all this land and all these trees. They are just stacked the length of…I can't even come up with how long they go on, and you found this tiny trail that weaves through them to this spot. How did you do that?"

He leaned his head to the left and shrugged. "We were gathering cattle one day, and I went in search for a calf and found him here. I roped him, but I had to pause and look around because this spot seemed to speak out to me. It hadn't been long since I'd come back from duty and had lost Darla. The peace of this place settled over me. So, I took the calf back and didn't say anything about this spot. Later that afternoon, I came here and sat there on that flat rock by the water. Many times over the years, it's been my thinking spot. Anyway, you asked for my favorite spot and this is it. I always thought if Darla had lived and then I found this spot, this would have been our place for picnics and romance. Then again, if I hadn't had such a sad feeling in my heart the first time I saw the place, it might not have made such a deep impression."

Her heart had begun hammering as his words had progressed. That was why he'd looked hesitant when she'd asked him to take her to his favorite place. She understood exactly how he felt. "Tucker, she would have loved it. It is so peaceful, beautiful, and like you said…romantic. You two would have had special moments here. I'm sure y'all would have come here often. Brought picnics and just enjoyed each other." Her head spun, thinking of the beauty that could come from this spot but the sadness that he'd had to use it for instead. "I love it too."

He turned toward the water, slightly away from her, and placed his hands on his hips as he looked out over the stream. "I don't see how anyone couldn't like it here. It's amazing. Even over there—see that pretty yellow flower growing across the stream on the edge of the water? There isn't much sun shining through the thick trees. Who knows, the flower might die tomorrow but today it's grown to that six-inch height and let those beautiful yellow petals fall open and it's facing our way, as if smiling. I've seen those off and on almost every time I've come out here. It's as if it's trying to uplift my spirits, in all honesty, though I haven't been out here in several long months."

"Why?"

"I've been contemplating trying to leave the past in the past and move forward. This might not actually be the past but it's where I spent so many hours thinking about the past."

Her heart hurt for him. "You didn't have to bring me here. I didn't want you to feel like you had to bring me someplace that would make you feel bad. I'm so sorry." She felt so horrible.

"It's all right. I'm glad I brought you out here. Maybe you'll be able to take this spot and in your book make it the spot I dreamed it would be. Give your hero and heroine a wonderful moment here. I mean, I'm not writing your book and I've never written a romance, but this could have been such a wonderful place to sit with your love. A happy, wonderous place for your main characters to visit. To have a special moment in time."

Oh yes, she could see it quite clearly. Too clearly. He turned his head and looked at her and her heart tightened—with sympathy. *Sympathy only.*

They stared at each other for a moment, then she forced a smile. "I can see exactly that. I'm going to make a promise to you that in this book, that will be a reality. They will have a special moment here. I can almost see it, but I don't have my hero and heroine quite developed yet. But this particular moment I can almost visualize and it will take readers' hearts soaring."

A soft smile developed on his lips and then slowly spread to a wide, amazing smile. "I think your readers will love it. If Darla was here, she would, too."

"I think Mark would agree. He loved forests, too. Even though we didn't live in the country, he loved them, so we have seen a successful scene. Forgive me for putting those two exact but different words together like that. They sound the same but are different."

"Kind of like our backgrounds of loss. Similar but different. Sorry, that may not make sense."

"I know what you're saying. Feeling. Our loss of our loves was different yet similar…especially the emotions we've sensed since losing them." She smiled weakly.

They had. "Exactly. My mother and her new husband, Seth, both know that feeling. Over time, they found each other and were able to have their past loves but find new love. I'm at that stage of hope for myself now, but I've just come to that place. It might not ever happen but I'm open to it, at last. Maybe in the next years, you'll reach that spot."

She took in his words but couldn't even imagine that coming true. "Or maybe I can just create those beautiful moments for my readers who need an escape."

WHAT A HEART'S DESIRE IS MADE OF

* * *

"Okay, then, I understand exactly where you're at. When you're ready to go to another spot, let me know. I've got a very happy and special place to show you. It's where, as far as I know, Nina and my brother first felt the move of strong attraction or even the move toward love."

"Now how can I turn that down? I want to see where Nina either began to fall in love with Jackson or did fall in love."

They looked around once more, then he led the way, making sure they didn't come across anything that could bite her or sting her. He opened her door and held her hand as she slid into the seat; then he closed it and strode to the driver's side. He was in no hurry for this day to end. There by the stream had a been a time of remembering pain but also of a moment of knowing it was time for him to move forward. But, even if the woman beside him now and who had been at the river with him moments before did attract him, she wasn't the one for him.

It was completely obvious that she wasn't interested in that way or ready to move forward. Only in this book she was writing. In her book, she was going to help others find escape from their sad moments. He hoped that in doing so she, too, would move a little forward in her time of learning to live again. Just like he was about to finally do after more years of sorrow than she'd yet lived through. For him, it was time to take a stand and begin again.

He pushed the gas and turned the truck and headed toward the lake. The lake Jackson had taken Nina to after they'd met, showing her places she could paint. Even though he'd done that, his brother hadn't gone into detail but Tucker was pretty sure his brother and Nina had had a very important moment here. Places for important moments was what Maggie needed for this book.

Green grass in a pasture with a cow might be important in some scenes, but they weren't the scenes where something really heart-grabbing would happen. But the lake and also the place they stood moments ago beside the stream were perfect.

When they reached the lake, she gasped as he pulled to a halt. "This is gorgeous. Nina painted this beautiful scene."

"Yes, she did. Did you see it?"

She grinned at him. "When I went to lunch with her at the house the other day, she showed me around and I noticed her beautiful painting in Jackson's office hanging over the fireplace."

"Exactly. It's a very important spot to them in their hearts. So I asked Nina if she'd mind me taking you here, and she'd thought it was a great idea. She said maybe you could use it because it was so important to her."

Maggie reached across the car seat and placed her palm on his wrist. "Thank you. I love it. Now let's get closer."

She let go of his wrist and he could feel the burning sensation that had started when she'd first touched him and now remained after she'd climbed from the truck. He forced himself to open his door, get out, and then met her at the front of the truck. He was getting himself into trouble, he worried.

She rushed down the path to the water's edge, and he followed at a slower pace. She stopped at the pretty lake's edge and he couldn't help noticing how it framed her beautiful figure. He was startled by acknowledging this. He might be ready to look for love but just looking at Maggie for any reason wasn't a good idea. Her words, the emotion he could hear at different times in her voice, told him she was nowhere close to being ready for what he was just now after all these years ready for.

She spun toward him, her eyes bright and beautiful with excitement. "I see it. I see the beginning of the scene." She pulled a small hand-sized notepad from her shirt pocket and tugged the tiny pen from its holder and jotted down words. He was fascinated by her actions and the joy he'd seen on her face. This was good for her. Nina had been right in getting her to come out here to the ranch. This beautiful ranch had been his healing place, both in peaceful beauty and in throwing himself into hard work. This was where he'd needed to be to find himself and now, he hoped…he prayed it was what this lovely lady needed.

"Do you ever swim here?" she asked, looking up suddenly.

"Um, yes. Well, not lately but when we were younger, we did a lot. Are you interested?"

She bit her lip. "Yes, but I'm not wearing a swimsuit today. I might come out another day and get the feel of the water."

"I'll bring you. I'd rather you not swim alone out here." He worried for her safety so he shoved the door shut on the desire to see her in a swimming suit.

"Thanks. Out here in the country by myself might not be a good idea, especially in the water. Do you ever see alligators?"

"Sometimes. You're smart. They move from the lake or pond, so they aren't always in one spot. No one has reported one in this one lately. So I think we're safe. I'll look around before we do any swimming, though."

"Thanks. You're very helpful. Okay, so where do we go next?"

He laughed, thoroughly enjoying her wish to see everything she could. "Well, you've seen a stream flowing beneath thick trees, a small lake situated in a peaceful rock-surrounded setting, and now you need to see something with hills? With expansive open fields?

Give me a hint." He grinned.

"Both. Just drive me around and let me look at this beautiful place today, and we'll do things like test the water on the next trip."

"Sounds good." He shifted his gaze from her to the water and studied it. "You know, this is a perfect place. I imagined many times of bringing Darla here and the two of us swimming and having a picnic. I didn't come out here for a while after I got back because of what I'd hoped to do here. Instead, I spent it at the stream I showed you earlier."

She was studying him and he suddenly wished he'd kept that to himself. *Why had he said that?* Yes, he'd hoped this would be a romantic, fun, memorial spot for him and his love. Instead, it had turned out to be that for Jackson and Nina. Now, maybe for many who would read Maggie's book it would make them smile, feel joy for her characters...maybe have hope for themselves. For him, he better get his thoughts back in place and stop sliding down the hill back into the darkness where he'd been.

Maggie placed her hand on his arm and squeezed

gently, startling him. "Maybe in your heart, this may one day be that happy place you wanted it to be. It seemed like the stream was the place you needed to be alone with your memories with Darla."

"Maybe so, but right now, I'm sorry I said that. This is the time for you to discover places to set your scenes for your book, not my past. Let's go see some more."

He led the way to the truck and they were back on track within a moment after they headed across the pasture. As the air flowed across them through the open windows, his spirit lifted again. When he glanced over at Maggie, she smiled, too, then stared back out the window, watching the acres pass by.

And so did he.

CHAPTER NINE

The day after she had gone on the tour with Tucker, Maggie was writing. They had ended the long, wonderful day before the sun set, and she had seen some beautiful country. But the first place he took her had such meaning and was her favorite spot. When she had gotten home, after telling him what a great day it had been, they had decided to go again—not today but tomorrow.

She'd been pleased because she'd wanted to write and she had, the moment she'd entered the house. She'd gotten herself a glass of water, pulled out a can of soup, heated it up, sat down and started working. Her mind rolled with inspiration from the day but particularly from spot where Tucker would go to mourn and try to figure his next steps of his life. That spot was going to be a romantic spot in the book like it should have been for him and Darla. It had been a wonder that Tucker had even taken her there, with how much the spot meant to him. But it meant a lot to her now, although probably not as much as it meant to him. He'd given her more motivation than she'd seen in this book, which she'd needed. Now, brain rolling, she started typing.

She'd written, actually written, the beginning scenes and she'd almost made the heroine the one who had lost her loved one. But she couldn't do that. She couldn't deal with her deep personal issues of loss but she could deal with the hero having lost his love, and she could have the heroine be the one who, while trying to help him, falls in love with him, and he does the same. Oh, it was going to be a good book but hard to write.

But like Tucker had said, he had decided after the years of mourning that it was time to make a point-blank decision by moving forward. She was nowhere near making that decision. But nothing said she had to wait as many years as he had to make that decision. But why was she even thinking that? She wasn't ready to think about ever falling in love again, so it was a weird thought rushing through her brain.

Finally, she turned the lights off and went to bed, determined to get going again tomorrow, and here she was now, working hard with her first cup of coffee beside her and her mind racing. She'd written a scene with the hero looking at the heroine for the first time and his heart had begun to pound...as had hers the first time she'd seen Mark.

Her phone rang and a glance showed it was Nina. She picked it up and pressed the Accept button. "Good morning."

"Not as good as it could be. Maggie, I'm having morning sickness right now, and I need to get over it because I'm going baby room shopping. I'd like to feel good picking out things for his room. Would you like to go and distract me from feeling ill when I'm supposed to feel enthusiastic and excited?"

Poor Nina. Morning sickness. "Sure, it sounds like fun and I want someone with you while you're feeling ill."

"Great. If you'll drive over here, then we'll go in my car."

"I'll be there soon. Maybe we should go in my car and I'll drive."

"Very well then. If you insist, that's what we'll do," she said with humor in her strained voice. "Just come when you're ready."

"I've been sitting here writing, so I need to add a bit of makeup and trade my pajamas for some shopping clothes. I'll see you within the hour."

"Great. Hopefully, I'll feel more like myself when you show up."

She hung up and hoped her friend got over the sickness soon. As odd as it seemed, envy radiated through Maggie at what Nina was feeling…it was something Maggie would most likely never feel.

Yet another depressing thought. She paused in front of the mirror and scowled at herself. "You have to move forward. Stop rolling in all the pain and loss, and just get moving."

She nodded in answer to her words, gave her reflection in the mirror a thumbs-up, and headed for her car. Helping Nina today would be a good thing.

Thankfully, Nina stood beside her front fence when Maggie drove up to the house, and she was smiling. Relief washed over Maggie at the smile.

"You look like you feel better," she said as she jumped from her car. "Am I right?"

"Yes, absolutely. I started feeling better about ten minutes ago. I think just knowing you were going with me did the job."

"That makes me feel good. So come on, climb in and tell me where to head."

"Let's go in my SUV, it'll hold more. We're heading through the crooked roads to Johnson City. Pretty country, nice town with a great baby store and then, before coming home, great places to eat."

She tapped the town into her phone's map. "Perfect. But I'll drive and you'll just sit back and relax. I'll get us there and then you can tell me where to take you."

"Sounds good." Nina led the way to the SUV and they took their seats. "Tell me how your exploring with Tucker went yesterday."

Maggie wasn't completely startled by the question

considering Nina had known she'd gone with him. She was startled by her friend's smile. She concentrated on getting the SUV down the drive heading toward the road. "It was beautiful and Tucker was really great. He told me about losing the woman he loved. I hadn't realized we had that in common. I hate it for him but he seemed to be adjusting. It's been a longer time from his loss to my loss, but he was inspiring. He's managed to find happiness again, it seems, and is finally going to look for love again."

"He told you all of that?" Nina gasped.

Maggie glanced at her. "Yes, we talked, and different things came out at different locations. But he told me that, I believe, trying to encourage me to take my time. Not to feel rushed by it but to work hard and keep busy until I'm ready for something different."

"Oh, I see. He's a great man and all of his brothers admire him, and they hated what he went through. They also backed off and let him mourn in his own way when he came home to the ranch. He did it alone and using hard work to keep him busy and distracted."

"I admire that they gave him his space. He seems

like a man who knows what he wants, and he goes and gets it. I have a feeling when he lost his love in a bombing, it was so very hard for a man like him. There was no going forward or controlling their relationship any longer and he needed space alone to come to grips with that."

Nina said, "Yes. How did you figure that out so quickly? I didn't. Jackson had to explain it to me."

"It fits him and until I came out here at your suggestion, it was something I wasn't doing. Sweet friends and neighbors were trying to pull me from my mourning and depression, my solitude, and I wasn't responding very well. I'm a strong person but losing my love…knocked me into the mud and I just couldn't come out for the longest time. But coming here, stepping forward was a new move for me. I came knowing I could hide and come out as I felt like it. You knew me and gave me a great inspiration by offering the quiet place that I can do that as needed."

"I'm so glad this is helping. I'm sad for you and Tucker both but glad you might be able to help each other."

"Me too. So far, I'm doing better than I expected. I wake up ready to work or like yesterday, explore. I loved that and I woke with words ramping to get out of my head this morning."

"Oh goodness, I'm sorry I called and interrupted—"

"No, don't apologize. I'm glad to spend time with you. I'll warn you there could be days when my spirits drop and I don't feel like meeting or doing something, but right now is not that time. To be honest, Nina, I feel Mark smiling and urging me to do this." She blinked back sudden tears and gently bit her lips to keep them from trembling.

"I know he is. That man of yours was always rooting for you. He loved you so very much. I have to be honest, since I met and fell in love with Jackson I know what that feels like now. Understanding how deeply you were loved now means more to me, and I know that wonderful man of yours would want you to find your happiness again. He'll always be by your side."

Maggie had pressed the brake and slowed the SUV

now as emotion and reality struck hard. She blinked back tears, gave her wonderful friend a quick glance, then went back to watching the road and making certain she didn't wreck them. That, for certain, Mark wouldn't want, considering that was how he was taken from her. "Yes, he would want me moving forward and I'm going to fight to give him what he would want. Even when it might be tough for me."

"That's my good friend talking. The one I love, and Mark loved."

Her insides cringed at the "loved" Nina had attached, unknowing how *loved* instead of *loves* hit her. He was no longer here so it was loved, but in her heart, he was still alive. "This is going to be a good day, and I can't wait to buy something or things for your sweet baby."

Nina smiled and leaned her head back. "I agree. I can't wait to hold him or her in my arms."

Maggie pushed her sorrow back and rejoiced for her friend. "I'm right there with you on that. I'll babysit anytime you need me to."

Nina sat up suddenly. "Are you thinking of moving

down here? That would be so wonderful. After all, with your writing career, you can live anywhere you like. There is no reason you have to live on those busy streets unless it's something you love."

Shock at her own words and now Nina's filled Maggie. *Did she want to move out into the country? To the quietness and serenity she could tell her friend felt?* "Actually, I might be considering it."

The idea and words stunned her. But she suddenly knew if her heart continued to feel stronger, this was indeed where she would move to…and maybe sooner than later.

* * *

"I like the way the room is turning out." Tucker placed his hands on his hips as he studied the pale yellow that he and Jackson had painted the baby's room.

Jackson grinned. "I do too. Nina said it would be like light-filtered sunshine of happiness every time we stepped in here, adding to the joy the gaze of our baby would give us when we picked him up and I agree wholeheartedly."

"Me too. I'm really looking forward to being an uncle again. I might drive you crazy, visiting and wanting to play."

"You are welcome anytime."

"Great. I'm counting on it." Tucker was drawn strongly to the idea of another baby in the family. The thought of having a baby of his own to love was one of the feelings pulling him to find love again. Having a family of his own was starting to swell in his heart. "You, my brother, are blessed."

Jackson reached out an arm and placed it on Tucker's shoulders, giving him a hug. "You were once and will be again. Now, let's go grab something to drink. I think our shoppers will be home soon and we might have to unload some things."

And he would get to see Maggie. Tucker had awakened this morning and headed to work early as usual but could tell by the light in the back of her cottage, in the kitchen, that she was up and probably having her coffee and opening her computer. Not a time to interrupt her, but he'd been slammed by how much he'd wanted to tell her good morning. How much he wanted to wish her a good day. Now he was going to see her.

Truth was, he needed to get this attraction he felt toward her under control. The last thing he needed was anyone seeing how she affected him after just meeting her.

He knew his family was rooting for him to find love again but being drawn strongly to someone who wasn't ready was not what he was going to do.

They were both drinking a glass of iced tea on the porch about six o'clock when Maggie drove Nina's SUV into the garage.

Jackson stood up after having waved at his wife in the passenger seat as they'd passed by. "Time to unload. Then we'll all have warmed-up burgers I made last night for tonight since I knew we were going to be busy."

"Sounds good." Tucker stood and followed his brother to the garage.

Nina had gotten out of the vehicle and beamed at them as Maggie rounded the front of the SUV. "Wait until you see what we picked out. It's going to make our sunlight baby room perfect."

Jackson pulled his wife into his arms and hugged her gently, then kissed her on top of the head. "I can't wait."

From behind her, Maggie's gaze met Tucker's as they both gave the soon-to-be parents the sweet moment. He gave a soft smile to her, hoping to not seem overly excited by the moment. She did the same. They were both clearly happy for Nina and Jackson.

"Okay," Jackson said, backing up and heading toward the back of the vehicle, where Tucker stood at the edge. "Let's open this up and see what we've got."

Nina moved forward and Maggie closed her door, after having sweetly told her she would do it. Now they all stood at the back as Jackson pushed the button and the big back end of the SUV lifted up, exposing a lot of large bags of things. They had definitely been buying and from the colors he could see at the top of some of the bags, they'd been buying colorful things.

"All right, this looks interesting, brother." He stepped up and reached for a big bag as Jackson also did.

"I can't wait to see, but we'll carry them upstairs to the room before we get to see what these two smiling ladies bought today."

"Sounds like a plan."

"Yes, because we want to see the room all painted," Nina said excitedly.

"It's all going to look wonderful," Maggie added. "I can't wait."

Moments later, after he and Jackson had piled as many bags in their arms as they could and Maggie did also, leaving only a big but lightweight bag for Nina, they all entered the pretty lemon-toned room.

"It's beautiful." Nina gasped.

"I agree." Maggie looked at the tone as the sun glinted softly through the window. "It's a happy, happy place."

He agreed wholeheartedly with her. But fought off meeting her gaze if she happened to look at him. Instead, he watched Nina accept Jackson's hug as he stepped behind her and pulled her against him with his hands crossing hers at her softly rounded stomach. His brother was where Tucker had hoped to be but wasn't; still, Tucker rejoiced at the love written all over them.

And then his gaze met Maggie's, and he could see

the happiness she felt for them. But the shadows within the depths of her soft-blue eyes were sad. He knew exactly why: her own dream of a child with the one she loved no longer existed, and he had the same knowledge. He and Maggie knew deeply how blessed Nina and Jackson were.

"Okay, time for you to see what we got." Nina moved forward and, with Maggie's help, tugged a plastic bag from the bag. They unzipped it then together pulled the pretty multi-colored baby blanket out, along with a royal-blue pillow with a kid in a cowboy outfit and another yellow pillow with a little cowgirl on it.

He grinned. "So do you keep both or the one that fits after you find out what you're having?"

"Yeah," Jackson said, his voice odd. "Or are you telling me we're having twins?"

Nina and Maggie both busted out laughing.

"I haven't decided how to handle it, but I can tell you that if we're having twins, I don't know it. It just came like this and we loved the colors. This is going to be a bright and happy place."

Jackson joined in the laughter and so did he. They'd

known how his brother would react and had enjoyed teasing him.

Both of the ladies then reached for bags and began pulling out a few baby clothes and colored baby towels and a few really cute stuffed toys. It was going to be a great room.

"I love it," he said, and looked from them to Jackson. "How about you?"

"I'm speechless and ready to play in here with my son. How about you, sweet soon-to-be mama?"

Nina blinked hard and her smiling lips wobbled. "I'm so ready."

Joy filled the room and Tucker smiled, feeling only happiness for them as his gaze locked with Maggie's again. Her eyes had only happiness for them also and they nodded in agreement.

CHAPTER TEN

"I love you." Seth slipped his arms around Alice after he'd helped her onto the large rock he stood on.

"Nothing makes me happier," Alice said and then looked out over the landscape. "This is so beautiful."

They'd spent the first couple of days of their honeymoon locked in their room at the beautiful hotel and loved every moment together. Now, they were starting to explore the area together, an island neither of them had been to before. This was their own new adventure and today, driving up to this lookout area showing the stunning green valley and the blue ocean it led to, was touching. Yes, they had ocean views back home on Star Gazer Island in Texas, but though she loved both places, this was different. This would always be where they'd spent their honeymoon.

"Are you having a good time exploring today?" He lightly kissed her forehead.

"I have, but only because I have you by my side." This wonderful man had filled in a vacant spot in her heart that, after losing her first love, she'd never expected could be filled. But she'd learned that a heart is a deep, beautiful place, and love could bloom inside it for someone new, while not knocking the love of her first love away.

"Once again, we agree. So, I guess we'll head down and we're going to that restaurant with music and dancing, and I'm going to hold you in my arms and enjoy the music with you."

"Perfect."

He moved off the boulder, put his hands around her waist and helped her down. Together, they wandered back down the passage and to where others were moving around from one lookout spot to the next.

"We were really lucky to have that moment alone."

"It looks that way. But even if we'd had other couples on that area while we were there, I was so absorbed by you being there with me as my wife that I wouldn't have noticed them."

Her heart squeezed. "You know how to make me feel wonderful." And it was true. Ever since they'd gotten married, then climbed onto the airplane and come to this beautiful place, he'd made her feel special and so very loved.

Tonight they'd be dancing under the moonlight, and she felt like she'd be doing that for the rest of her life with Seth.

* * *

Lisa closed the doors to the kitchen on Saturday. A week without Alice had kept her busy, making sure the inn and the restaurant flowed well. Thankfully, all the women who worked at the inn were good at what they did and out to make sure Alice had nothing to worry about. She'd had the help of Zane in the kitchen, he was so very good. The man stepped in many times, giving her time to go check on the customers, not just those sitting at the tables in the dinner or patio but the ones coming and going from the inn. She'd been able to take care of so much, but really with the good help Alice had hired and the good help she'd hired in the kitchen, the week had run smoothly so far. All except her thoughts going continually to the boat ride and the talk she and Zane had shared…and the hug, the embrace, and the fact that she'd wanted him with all of her being to kiss her. But he hadn't.

Now, she was tired because she hadn't taken any actual breaks all week, and neither had Zane. The man had insisted on being there as her backup, knowing the pressure she felt to make sure Alice had no surprises when she and Seth arrived home in four days.

Zane had been perfect. She started to walk across the path toward her house, having told him he didn't need to wait on her, so go home and get some rest. He'd done it, but as she reached the cute red house that she now called home, he sat on the tailgate of his truck, watching her approach.

"Zane, what are you doing?" she asked, to which he

smiled, sending unwanted zings and sparks flashing through her.

"I left work like you suggested and came over to my friend's house to see if she felt like taking a walk on the beach?"

She didn't miss his highlight of "friend's" house and it touched her deeper that he was trying to be the man she needed him to be. Not the man he knew she wasn't looking for, or at least wasn't ready for. "I'm tired, but actually a casual stroll out there on this beautiful night sounds great. I need to unwind."

"Me too." He slid from the tailgate then closed it before walking with her to the house.

She unlocked the door and he followed her inside and into the kitchen. The room seemed smaller as his presence filled in around her. She was becoming overwhelmed by the way he drew her. "I'll change quickly. Grab something to drink if you want it and wait in the house or on the back patio."

"Will do."

She hurried into her bedroom and quickly changed from her work outfit to her long shorts and T-shirt.

WHAT A HEART'S DESIRE IS MADE OF

Carrying her flip-flops into the kitchen, she found him standing with his back to the room as he stared out at the ocean. The man was wonderful to look at. As he turned toward her, she had to force her eyes away as she sat on one of the chairs at the table and slipped her flip-flops on. "I'm not wearing shoes since walking fast is not on my list tonight."

He grinned. "Fine with me. We'll go at whatever pace you want to go. You've got to be tired. You haven't stopped once this week."

She stood and he opened the door; they walked out onto the patio, then to the gate and out onto the sand. "I haven't, but it's been worth it. I couldn't have done it without you, Zane. Seriously, knowing you are there in the kitchen when I was out checking all different things helped. Though I have to say that Alice did a wonderful job hiring help and they have done great this week. I feel a bit bad checking on them so much but have to remind myself that it's about the customers. I'm pleased to say they've all talked about how amazing the service is and the restaurant also."

"That's not all just because of Alice. She's amazing

but so are you. Don't forget that. I can promise you Alice knows that and probably hasn't worried one instant about this place."

They'd reached the water's edge and she stopped and breathed in the air. "Again, I couldn't have done it without you. Isn't it a gorgeous night? Like a prize after a busy week."

"Very beautiful and definitely a prize."

His deep voice drew her gaze. He stared at her, not the water, and every goose bump she had and more popped to standing at seeing the emotion in his eyes.

Lisa shivered and looked back out at the dark water rolling in, and her mind rolled right along with it. She swallowed hard, hoping to calm her reaction to this handsome man.

"I didn't mean to upset you," Zane said gently as he stepped to stand beside her. His shoulder grazed her ever so slightly and sent more shivers racing through her.

She tried to step away, but her feet refused to move. She was tired, so tired, and that was to blame for her reactions. But deep down she knew that wasn't the case.

She was reacting to him this way because she was so drawn so powerfully to this man. "Y-you didn't upset me. I'm glad to be here with you." And she meant it.

"You just made my year. I don't want to cross any lines you've drawn, but I'd like to hold you again, give you support. If you have a problem with that, just say no."

The man always asked and she wasn't sure whether it was because she was his boss or he was just trying to give her the power over their relationship. Whatever it was, she suddenly couldn't stop herself as she stepped forward into his wonderful arms. Instantly, they wrapped around her and held her close to his pounding heart. She laid her head on his chest. Emotions swept through her as her arms tightened around his waist and wished to be around his neck, pulling his lips to hers—*what?* She lifted her head and met his gently penetrating gaze. Her heart thundered as they stared and then, unable to stop herself, she lifted her lips and kissed him.

***

Zane had wanted to hold Lisa all week and had worked

hard to keep himself in his place as her support chef. She'd done a wonderful job and he'd been able to tell by her sincere eyes that he was helping her make it through Alice and Seth's honeymoon time. All week long, he'd begun to know that his own dream was a honeymoon week or life with Lisa. He was in rough waters.

He let her soft lips take his and held back the need he had to show her how much he cared for her by deepening their kiss. Emotions that were assaulting him and he fought hard to not over-respond and scare her. But then she pulled an arm from his waist and slid it around his neck, her fingers gently tugging him closer. *Did she know what she was doing to him?* The question raced through him but he'd already reacted, deepening his kiss and feeling her respond with just as much enthusiasm as he was giving her.

Finally, as if they both came to their senses at the same time, they pulled their lips apart and stared at each other. He feared he'd messed up royally. This was a beautiful, life-changing kiss to him, a man who'd wished for this all of his life, but he'd moved too fast and he knew he was about to be pushed away. He had to take the blame, save her from feeling bad. "I didn't mean to do that."

She blinked. "I started it. I'm sorry."

"Nothing for you to be sorry for. I honestly loved it. But I didn't mean to lose control and make you feel bad. I can see it in your eyes."

She stepped back. "Zane, I'm just so confused. I have been ever since I hired you but more since our boat ride. I think about you often, even when I shouldn't."

He wanted to draw her back into his arms but held back. The thing he'd found from the kiss was that she might be trying to stay apart from him, but she did have feelings for him. He had to proceed cautiously. "Are you going to let your ex-husband control your life forever?"

Her eyes flared. "He isn't controlling me. I'm controlling me."

"So you aren't letting his ridiculous actions keep you away from having a fulfilling life with..." He stopped himself before he went too far, saying *true love*. He loved her but she wasn't ready to hear that and might not ever be ready. "Whatever you want."

"This is not the relaxing walk we'd planned. I think it's time to go home."

She turned and strode back toward her house, and he fell into step with her. He'd messed up, but the feel of her lips and the emotion and reactions in her kiss had been beautiful until she'd pulled back. Tonight had been a mistake. A big mistake that he might never fix. She might even ask him to find a new job.

* * *

Inside her house, Lisa threw her back against the door and listened to Zane drive away. Tears welled in her eyes. She slammed them shut and fought not to cry. It didn't work as the engine sound disappeared in the distance and she saw Zane disappearing in her life. *Was that what she wanted?*

Oh, how she wished Alice was here to talk to. She needed someone to talk to but she had no one she trusted with this except Alice. However, this would not be fair to share when her friend arrived home from her honeymoon because Alice would soaring with well deserved happiness and Lisa wouldn't do anything to bring that down with her emotional state. She had to get her head on straight and appear fine and in control when Alice arrived.

Her only worry was that now, after having shared that powerful kiss, could she and Zane go back to just working together? She hoped so because it suddenly slammed into her that him leaving the restaurant would be hard for her to endure and it had nothing to do with him not being there to help her cook.

CHAPTER ELEVEN

Tucker followed Maggie home after they'd eaten dinner with Jackson and Nina. She had enjoyed herself but he'd seen emotion in her expression at times when the expectant parents' love was so visible. He'd been there and still was, but not so deeply. *Why was that?*

He'd loved Darla desperately, so was he heartless to not feel as deeply connected as he had? Moving forward had just in the last couple of months taken hold after all this time since he'd lost her, and he'd grabbed hold of it and was now hoping for love again. But seeing the emotion of Maggie's love for Mark set him back tonight.

He pulled the truck in behind her but didn't get out. He'd rolled his window down and now leaned his head out as she climbed from her car. "I'll watch you get in and then head down to my place. Do you need anything?"

She hesitated and then walked toward him, stopping just past his mirror. "They are such a happy couple. Seeing them together makes me happy for them and sad for my loss. I hope that didn't show to them. I tried not to show it."

"They would understand if they were looking at you in their moments of joy they kept sharing. But they were looking at each other, so your moments of sadness were missed by them."

She looked away and took a deep breath. "I guess they weren't from you?"

"No. I caught them because I looked away from them, to give them those moments together, and my gaze always went to you first."

She looked back at him. "I hope you're right. I don't want to put sadness on top of this wonderful time for them."

"You're not. Nina is glad you're here and it was evident you two had fun shopping today. Although I was surprised when Jackson told me you were with her. I thought you were going to hole up and put words on paper today." That got him a smile and he was glad.

"I had—or I was writing when she called but there was no way I wasn't going with her after she told me she was having some morning sickness. I really enjoyed it, and she started feeling better fairly quickly so we had a great day."

"Good. So my suggestion to you now is don't let sorrow overtake your happy moments. You know your husband would want you to have happiness again. I have a feeling he loved you so much that he's rooting for you."

She smiled as she stared at him. "I truly believe you're right. Thank you for the reminder and I am trying to let happy moments shine. I have a feeling you had as hard a time as I'm having but you're now doing well."

"Yes. I've had longer but I know a lot of people who haven't needed as much time as I had. I'm not sure what the difference is but I think it's because the right person comes along when the time is right."

"Maybe a God thing," she offered. "I'll head in now. Sleep good." She turned and headed toward the porch.

"I hope you sleep good, Maggie. Let me know when you're ready for another exploring adventure."

She turned back to look at him and smiled. "I will. But tomorrow is definitely a writing day. Goodnight."

He watched and was glad he'd helped her focus on something other than the loss of her husband. At least he thought he'd helped. He hoped he'd helped.

When he got to his cabin, he strode from the living space to the kitchen and then back again, feeling really restless. He headed out onto the patio and stood at the edge with his hands on his hips as he stared out into the darkness…the quietness. This had once been the only way he could deal with his broken heart: just him and the stillness and silence. But tonight there was nothing about it that he liked. He shifted to the other side of the patio. From there, he could see Maggie's cabin. Her kitchen lights were on and so was the outside patio light. *Was she out there?* He couldn't see her but knew she could be sitting in the shadow of the table and its umbrella.

Was she sad? Did she need comfort? Did she need someone to show her that life could begin again? He wanted to be that person—

What he was letting happen was ridiculous. He was falling for her and needed to move back. Needed to stop what he was feeling or he could make a mess out of her emotions and life. Might mess up their friendship…even though he knew now without doubt that he was wanting more than just a friendship with Maggie. He rammed a hand through his short hair, knocking his hat off since he'd forgotten he hadn't taken it off. Reaching down, he swept it off the porch and headed inside. It was time to shower and get some sleep…if he could. He had serious doubts that he'd get any.

***

The following day, Tucker drove to Star Gazer Island and pulled up to the feed store. He needed some new bottles for the calf that had been born during the night. They'd found it early after knowing the cow was expecting and finding her wandering around in the pasture alone. He and one of the workers had driven through the pasture in hunt for the calf that had obviously been born but was nowhere near the mom. They found it at the back of the pasture in a dip, looking as if it had been neglected not long after arriving. Quickly, they'd taken her back to where the mother cow was but she ignored her. So they were giving it a little more time but then he was going to start feeding it and a new bottle would help. He got everything he needed then headed for his truck.

"Hey, big brother," the familiar voice of his brother Riley called out.

He turned and found him striding toward him from down the sidewalk. "Riley, good to see you."

Riley came up and gave him a quick hug. "You haven't been out to the camp since Mom and Seth got married. What's up?"

He'd spent some time out there helping Riley get the camp ready for groups and had promised to help out whenever he was needed. "Sorry. Have you needed me? I've been a little busy at the ranch and—"

"And helping out with the visitor on the ranch? Jackson told me you have a neighbor right now and you were being very helpful."

"I help when she needs it."

Riley's smile widened. "Bring her out to the camp. He said she was a writer friend of Nina's. She might find something out about the camp she might want to put in her book. As you know, Sophie and I are having a great time out there."

He grinned. "You two would have a great time anywhere. When are y'all setting a date?"

"Soon, actually. We were just waiting for Mom and Seth to tie the knot and now we're going to let all of you in on our plan. It's going to be quiet and with no show. So be ready because one day you'll get the invite and boom! She and I will be a married happily-ever-after couple." Riley smiled almost from ear to ear with happiness.

Tucker laughed and raised a knotted fist of triumph. "This is going to be great. I'm so happy for you both and when you send out that invite, I'll be there."

"Great. Stay tuned, brother and when the time comes, bring a date if you want to." He winked. "Okay, gotta go get these supplies out to the camp. Again, come on out any time. Ride a horse on the beach or sit around the campfire. We'll be glad to see you anytime."

"I'll let you know. You've made my day, I'm thrilled for you two."

Tucker watched his smiling brother climb into his truck, back out, and head down the street. He was so happy for these two and couldn't wait to celebrate his last brother to get married. Of course, he would be their last brother to get married—if he ever found another perfect woman for himself.

Maggie's smiling face flashed across his eyes…he shut it down. Not the thing to keep thinking about. He was simply the cowboy sometimes showing her places that might make a great scene for her romance novel—not the star of her story. Again, he reminded himself, she might one day get to where he was, looking to fill the space his lost love had filled. But she was not there yet, and he was not the man who would test the waters.

His phone rang and to his surprise, it was none other than Maggie. He instantly pushed Accept. "Good morning."

"Hi. I'm sorry to bother you but I got up early this morning and have really been typing out crazy fast. The book is flowing but I hit a scene where a baby calf is being bottle fed and I've never seen a live viewing, only videos. You don't happen to have or know someone who has one they're feeding, do you? I'd love to see it first-hand before I write the scene."

He was speechless for a moment. "This is really wild. Freaky, actually. See, I'm in town and just picked up a new bottle because we have a new calf born last night and the mother refused to feed her, so I'm about to head back to the ranch and feed it. I can come by and pick you up or you can meet me at the smaller barn across the drive from Nina and Jackson's house."

"This is wonderful. I'll meet you there. Are you on your way now?"

"Just got in the truck. Be there in about twenty minutes. So no rush for you since you're closer."

"See you soon. I'm so excited."

He chuckled and they hung up. He knew he was probably about to get into dangerous waters. Just her voice had set his adrenaline pumping.

He thought about her all the way home. Trying to talk himself down from the exhilaration her excitement had shot into him.

She had just pulled in close to the barn when he drove up beside her. She was out of the car before he was and smiling with that contagious enthusiasm. He'd grown so used to ranching and delivering baby calves that it had been a very long time since he'd experienced this feeling. He smiled as he climbed out, happy to relive through her the fun and happiness saving a calf from starvation could be.

"You've made this morning turn into one of pure pleasure. Let's go feed a calf and keep her alive."

"Yes, I'm so glad you found her."

He started toward the open barn door with her beside him. "I am too. Sometimes this happens. We try to keep a good watch on all pregnant cows, but we have a lot, and this one happened in the night, so we had to search for it after realizing the mother had given birth and was not doing her job, caring for her baby."

"Is that her?" she asked, spotting the baby curled up inside a stall.

"Yes. Thankfully, she's the only one right now. We have had to save more sometimes. Let me get the bottle mixed up and ready. You can watch if you'd like."

"Yes, please." She followed him to the area where they kept all the supplies.

Maggie waited as Tucker opened the gate and walked into the stall first. He held the gate for her and she passed in front of him, her gaze on the little ball of fur and legs still curled up. She stopped and waited as he shut the gate and moved to crouch down beside the baby.

He placed a hand on the very still but breathing baby then looked up at Maggie. "You can come here beside me and bring the bottle."

She crouched down beside him, clutching the bottle to her chest. "Is she going to be okay?"

"Yes, we just gave her mother a shot at helping her and it didn't happen, so while I was getting the supplies in town, my helper brought her here. He'd been watching while I left, hoping the mother would come to her senses. But it didn't happen, so here we are."

He was rubbing the calf's head and it opened its eyes. "This sweet calf looks sad and weak, and it's pushing at my heart."

"The little ones can do that. Give her a drink and all will be better."

"Do I put the nipple of the bottle to her lips?"

"Yes, gently, and see if she catches on fast. If she doesn't, then keep on touching her lips and push it toward her teeth. She'll catch on."

She did what he'd instructed. After rubbing the nipple across the calf's lips several times, Tucker then placed his fingers against hers and pressed slightly so the bottle slipped past the lips and the calf's teeth. The calf opened up and took the end of the bottle and immediately started sucking the milk.

"Awesome," Maggie whispered excitedly and looked at Tucker.

He loved her excitement. "You did great. Just thought I'd give you a little help on getting a reaction from this little gal. You're her best buddy now."

Her smile grew as she looked from him to the baby and then back at Tucker. "This is so great. I haven't felt any joy like this in so very long. Amazing to think, feeding a calf is bringing me so much joy."

"Saving the life of a calf. You're doing wonderful. I'm glad you called. I should have called you just in case you might be interested. But I do find it wild the coincidence of this baby needing some love and you feeling the need to put one in your book at the same time. You can come feed her anytime you feel like it." Still gently holding her hand he now pulled it away, missing the feel of her instantly.

"I might show up every day," she warned.

Sounded good to him. "We feed several times a day, so you don't have to come first thing in the morning. I'll give you times and all you have to do is let me know when you want to come and I'll have it ready for you."

"I'll be taking you up on that." Her eyes sparkled and dug into his.

He could see her excitement as if the entire idea of feeding this sweet little calf and watching her grow stronger every day was the best thing ever. Suddenly he hoped some of her excitement might involve spending time with him too. Tucker tried to remain calm. "Great. But, I know you have writing to do, so don't let it get in the way. We still have more ranch to see, and a swim in the lake to enjoy. If you're having a swimming scene, you need to feel the water around you."

Her cheeks turned pink as if blood was rushing through her. It slammed into him, having been so long since he'd felt these feelings of emotion…of attraction…and she froze suddenly as their gazes locked and she looked almost as if she felt what he felt and was shocked.

"Sorry, if that was too, um, over the line. I didn't mean to—"

"No, I didn't take it wrong. I just overreacted. I would love to go. You just tell me when. I'll write extra hard this afternoon and in the mornings, and be ready for as much experience here on the ranch as you can show me. Readers will love it. At least, I hope."

"Then I'll set it up for tomorrow. My mom is arriving back then and the day after we're all going to throw them a welcome home party at Jackson's home, so I won't be available that day."

The calf yanked on the bottle, clearly starting to get into getting the milk. She looked away from him and made sure the bottle was still in place. "Tomorrow is perfect. I'm excited for y'all getting to celebrate the newlyweds' arrival home. Soon I'm going to go check out her beautiful bed-and-breakfast and have a meal there."

"I'd be glad to take you. For research, of course." He hitched a brow and hoped, as she hesitated that she said yes...

* * *

Maggie couldn't speak as she met Tucker's teasing eyes. The man had drawn her in with his invitation to take her swimming and show her whatever she needed. "Research it certainly will be, because it sounds like some of my characters might come as visitors to the one in my book, if I put something like that in the book."

"Then we'll set that up. Also, my brother Riley—I

saw him this morning in town—said to bring you out to the camp he and his fiancée are running together. He thinks you'll like it and it might be a good place for a scene."

"You are good at this, Tucker. That would be a great place to see."

"Then it sounds like the next week is going to have several fun experiences in it."

"Yes." Her heart paused and her world spun a bit. This was starting to sound wonderful but also shaky. She realized the shaky part was because looking at Tucker was pumping up the feelings of attraction she hadn't had for anyone other than her Mark.

And she wasn't sure at all how she felt about it. Shock. Interest. Excitement…or any of the other feelings that were suddenly rushing over her like a huge ocean wave. *What was going on?*

She wasn't sure, but the most odd thing of all was the feeling of Mark walking up behind her, slipping his arms around her, and dipping his lips to her ear and whispering, "Don't back down. Move forward."

The words vibrated through her, and she focused

back on the calf and the now empty bottle. "It's gone," she said, relieved to have something to focus on than her raging emotions.

"Great. Tug it out and let's see if we can get this little gal standing."

She did as he said, and he took the bottle and set it on the top of the wood railing. Then, as she stood up, he reached down and lifted the calf to a standing position. It stumbled then gingerly touched her hooves to the ground and balanced with a stumble and then legs wide apart. It was adorable and sent thrills through her. This calf was overcoming and going to do great.

"I'm so happy to see her fighting to stand like that." She clasped her hands tighter under her chin and smiled as she pushed back tears of happiness.

"You helped her, and I hope it is what you needed for your book this morning."

She realized it could have meant a lot more than just a great scene for her book. Like this calf, she would overcome and with the push from her sweet husband and Tucker, she would move forward. She would.

CHAPTER TWELVE

Tucker buried himself in work after Maggie headed back to her cabin to get back to writing her book. He'd needed physical work to try to ease the conflict fighting inside him. The pull he felt for her was strong, and it had been crazy of him to place his hand over hers when she'd been holding that bottle for the calf. He hadn't removed it for a while and she hadn't seemed to mind his hand being there.

But he couldn't let this draw he felt toward her get him into a situation that caused him to bring emotional pain to this beautiful woman trying to overcome her sorrow of loss. She wasn't ready.

He repeated the words over and over in his head,

and his thoughts finally, late in the day, registered on Seth. Seth had suffered the loss of his beloved wife to cancer and had moved to Star Gazer Island afterward and had been here living a life like Tucker: full of work and silence in the evenings and nighttime as he couldn't move forward. But then coming to the inn to apply for the remodeling job, he'd met Tucker's mom. They'd both come from grieving heartbreak; they'd been drawn together and were now starting over in love again. Seth had lost his wife a few years before his mom had lost his father, and Seth had fallen first and kept his love to himself to give Tucker's mom time to find her footing again and then fall for him also.

The thought slammed into Tucker as almost a similar romance plot...now he was thinking like Maggie the romance writer with thoughts of a romance plot...but it fit. More startling was the fact that he'd just thought of Seth falling in love and waiting on his mother, and Tucker felt the same way. He had somehow, at some point, with a little time alone with her, fallen in love with Maggie.

He straightened to a full standing position from the

bent-over position he'd been in, fixing a fence wire. He'd driven out here alone after his mind had started to spin. Now he stared out across the open pasture as the reality hit him with that "fallen in love with Maggie" thought. He was in love again and had no idea whether Maggie would ever be ready for love again or not.

He needed to talk to his new stepfather. The loss of his own dad filled him as it sometimes did when he needed advice his dad wasn't here to give. But Seth was, and he would completely understand. He already knew from just watching Seth that he would tell him to just be there for her and give her the room she needed to overcome her sorrow and heal in her own time.

The emotion of the whole situation slammed into him: his loss of his father, loss of his first love, and now the fact that he had quickly and unknowingly fallen in love with a beautiful, loving woman in her own pain who might never want to remarry.

He wiped the tear off his cheek and gritted his teeth as he forced himself to give up the sorrow rolling through him. He would figure this out. He would be strong and he would take whatever came from this.

Now, to make it through swimming in the lake with Maggie. He was going to have to use every muscle in his body and mind to keep his feelings hidden and his arms from winding around her and pulling her close.

* * *

Maggie climbed from the truck as soon as Tucker pulled to a halt at the beautiful small lake that was the subject of one of Nina's amazing paintings. Nina had created a painting with the romance and peace the place provided, and now Maggie was wanting to place a special time here in her book. She could see her two characters swimming together in the water and she was about to feel it against her skin. With Tucker beside her.

"Are you ready?" He came up beside her and handed her a towel. "You forgot this."

"Thanks. My mind went to the water and the surroundings and my book. Let's go feel the water on our skin so I can relay it to my readers." She smiled at him and the sudden grin he gave her told Maggie that he was as excited as she was about doing this.

"Here we go. It's been a long time since I swam here. Me and my teenaged brothers back then did flips from those rocks into the water." He pointed ahead of them to the rocks beside the water. "Are you ready to try?"

She laughed at the teasing in his voice. "You know I'm not. I can see you and all of your brothers doing that, though."

They'd reached the section to walk down the slope to the water's edge and he held his hand out to her. "We loved it, but I can promise you I won't be doing that today."

She slipped her hand into his. "Good. I can relax then." His fingers were warm as they wrapped around hers, and he led her down the path, making certain that if she slipped, he could catch her. She liked the feeling and knew that would be in the book for her heroine.

"Please relax and enjoy yourself. I wouldn't want you coming out here alone and swimming just in case something happened. You know, a cramp or—well, you never know. It's always good to have someone near you when in the water."

They'd reached the water's edge and he released her hand then laid his towel on the large flat rock by the water. Her mind stuck on his words as she laid her towel beside his then touched his arm. "You're thinking about your dad."

He nodded. "Yes. A few of the hands were already across the river and the water wasn't hugely deep. It was just rushing, with the flooding coming down it. Dad was ahead of me and my brothers as he took some cattle across the river. Something in the water gave way, or where he entered was just deeper and the strength of the water swept him and his horse under. Dad came up briefly, then was dragged under and we never saw him alive after that. Jackson was the closest to him. In that situation, a flowing flooded river with trees and limbs and no telling what all was washing down the river just beneath the water—it's dangerous. Dad got caught up in downed tree limbs and even he, the strong man that he was, didn't make it."

"I'm so very sorry." Her heart clenched tightly at the sorrow in his words.

"I am, too. I don't know about you, but I've learned that we all have a time to be called home and that was

Dad's time. Me and my brothers cherish the time we had with him and are grateful for every moment. Even the times when we were in trouble, and he was being a good father by setting us straight." He smiled slightly. "He was good and taught us well."

She took in his words. "So, you think despite it being an accident that no matter what, that was just his time to go?" She crossed her arms and her hands clung to her forearms.

"I do. I never talk about this, but I had a lot of close calls when I was in the Marines. A lot. There were several times I shouldn't have come out alive, but I did while others didn't. Darla actually helped me through a rough time after many of my division were killed and I was just grazed by a shot. I felt terrible because I was alive and they weren't. She's the one who pointed out that she believed we each have a time. Not everyone believes that, but she did, and after she was killed in that bombing…I struggled hard with it. But she kept coming to me in thoughts and dreams telling me it was her time. She was always smiling and telling me everything was wonderful."

"Wonderful?"

He smiled at her. "She, too, was a Christian and believed she had a real home to go to…one day I'll see her again. My father also."

Maggie's heart surged, and she closed her eyes as she felt Mark's warm, wide smile shine down on her in the sunshine glistening on the lake. She blinked slowly, feeling the tears smooth out that she'd felt coming. "You have helped me so many times since I moved into the cabin near yours. I can feel my sweet Mark agreeing with you. He wants me to move on."

"To carry him in your heart but find a new life? That's what I feel from Darla. It took me a while to be able to start thinking about actually doing it like I am now. But it's been longer for me, and you may still have a path to go down to be able to do that. It's understandable."

He was right but looking at him, her heart skipped several beats. He was a great guy. A wonderful man. She looked out at the water. "Okay, it's time to test out this water." Without even thinking about it, she tugged her shirt off over her head and tossed it to the rock. Then she unzipped her cotton shorts and stepped out of them.

Her black one-piece had nice coverage and she knew she wasn't overexposed, but if she hadn't hurried taking off the coverup clothing, she wouldn't have done it. Without taking a glance at Tucker, she stepped into the water and let the feel of the slick mud and rock variation tickle the bottom of her feet. She really didn't like the feel that much but just a few more steps and she'd be in deeper water. Suddenly there was a splash beside her and the next thing she saw, a few feet ahead of her, was a wet Tucker coming up from the water.

He grinned. "I'd rather drench myself instantly instead of walking slowly to the deeper area."

She laughed. "I wish I'd have thought of that but then, I wasn't sure of the depth. Obviously, you are."

He held his hand out to her. "Yes, I brought you to this side because it does deepen quicker than the other areas. I didn't feel like you'd want to stand around or walk around in knee-deep water. Give me your hand, and I'll give you a quick tug off the slimy bottom. If you can keep yourself afloat."

She laughed and slipped her hand into his. In a split second, she was three feet farther into the lake and using her moving legs to keep her afloat. He let go of her hand and she gently waved them around in the water and stared across the water at him. He was so good-looking and likeable. She couldn't figure out why women hadn't been chasing him down. Or trying to. Of course, she was startled that she was even thinking such a thing.

"What are you thinking about?" he asked.

"Nothing, um, just that this is a beautiful lake, or huge pond. I'm really not sure what to call it." She yanked her gaze off him and swirled so she looked about the lake from inside the lake rather than from the shore. Anything to not be looking into his eyes.

"I call it a lake. A pond is smaller and, as far as I'm concerned, round and good for a cow to enter and cool off. This lake doesn't draw the cattle too much because of the depth and the rock. At least that's what I've always believed."

She heard a small splash and looked over her shoulder to see that he was gone. She spun looking for him, and then spotted him bob up out of the water several feet away, toward the middle of the lake. Relief washed through her. "You scared me. I thought something had happened."

He leaned his head to the side. "I'm fine. Sorry to have scared you. Swim out here and join me. Are you getting any ideas for how to use the swimming lake in your book?"

She swam toward him, startled to realize she hadn't been thinking about her book. Just him. "Oh, you know, a romantic moment for the stars of the book. Maybe a turning point."

Tucker waved his muscled arms through the water around him. "Perfect spot for that. Will they kiss for the first time here?"

Her gaze locked on his, and she told herself not to think about where her mind had just gone. *What would it be like to kiss Tucker?*

This was not good. "No. I don't think so."

"Then will it happen later in the book, or maybe the second time they swim together?"

This really was not good. Her mind whirled around thoughts of her characters kissing but the reality was, she was thinking again of *them* kissing. "I don't know. I'll come up with it."

"Maybe you can put a scene in of them swimming in the bay when you see it from the campgrounds. Riley and Sophie have invited us out to the camp. It's interesting. Might set you up for a great scene. The ocean versus the lake."

"I'd like to take a look."

"Great. They want to meet you. That's where all the magic of their relationship developed, so maybe you can get some ideas from them."

"Maybe. I think I'm ready to stop bobbing up and down and get out of the lake for now."

"Sounds good. Head in and I'll follow you. Or if you don't want to touch the lake bottom, I'll carry you out."

His words shocked her. No way did she need him carrying her out of the water. As of right now, the way he was starting to affect her was disturbing enough. She would probably not be wanting to let go of him if he carried her from the water. "I'll swim. See you at the shore." And then she spread her arms out, kicked her feet back behind her rather than beneath her, and she swam for the shore. Seconds later, her feet were in the grassy mud again, but she ignored the feeling and strode toward the shore and the rock that held her towel and her clothes.

He was suddenly walking beside her, his strong, lightly hairy chest glistening with water in the sunlight. Her heart hammered as she met his gaze. Quickly, she looked back at the shore just two steps away and tripped on a large rock. She gasped as she fell forward but was instantly swooped up into Tucker's muscled arms and held against his chest.

"Are you all right?" He stared into her eyes, looking as stunned as she felt.

"Yes," she breathed out. Her heart pounded as she took in the feel of his arms holding her and the look in his eyes. "Fine. I-I can walk. It was a big rock."

"Glad I was there to catch you." He took the last two steps and they were on the shore.

But to her dismay, he didn't put her down, just stared at her. She couldn't tear her eyes away.

His gaze dropped to her lips—instantly, her gaze dropped to his lips.

What was she doing?

"I need down," she blurted out and wriggled, and he immediately set her feet upon the ground.

"Steady." He held her arms for a second longer, then let go.

"Thanks." Her voice was embarrassingly shaky. She reached for her towel and immediately dried her hair and then wrapped the towel around her body to soak up the water and cover her up, suddenly feeling completely exposed. *What had happened?*

"What's wrong?" Tucker asked, letting her know that her face showed she was disturbed.

"Nothing. Well, I haven't been in a man's arms in a very long time. Especially a man other than Mark. It disturbed me." She looked at him then and saw the realization in his eyes.

"I didn't mean to upset you."

That was the problem. It hadn't upset her in the way he was assuming. It had upset her because she reacted in the way of a woman drawn to a man. "It's all right." Frustration washed over her, and she spun, grabbed her shorts and shirt, and started up the hill. She just had to put space between them. She was not in a place she was ready to be in.

Was she?

* * *

Tucker couldn't move as he ran through her words again. She'd reacted to being in his arms and he felt like it had been in a good way. But that was what had put her in such turmoil. Joy leapt through him at the thought, then he slammed it down. He didn't want to cause her any more pain. He'd slid into this readiness in a long length of time—seven years—which she hadn't had. Two maybe, was all. He would have been completely torn up then too.

He grabbed his pants and shirt and towel, too, and hurried behind her. "I'm here if you need help on the hill."

"I'm fine. But thanks."

He wrapped the towel around his waist and wet swim trunks. He'd had a heck of a time getting his pants on over the trunks and knew there was no way it was going to happen over the wet one. He followed her to the truck and tossed his clothes into the backseat while she pulled open her door and tossed her towel in and yanked her shirt on, then her shorts.

He closed the back door and placed a hand on her door. "Maggie, you've done nothing wrong. Try to calm down and not get so upset about this."

She raked a hand through her hair and stared out across the pasture. She looked so stressed and...sad. "He's only been gone two years. Yes, you are a wonderful man, but that I reacted like this with you now is just not right."

What did he say to that? He was happy that she was reacting to him but understood her emotions. "I'll start staying away from you, if that's what you want."

"No, I didn't mean I wanted to end our friendship. I'm just confused by what I'm feeling."

His heart ramped up. "What are you feeling?"

She stared at him. Her eyes dimmed, and she paled. "I need to head back to the house." She slid onto the passenger's seat and stared out the front window.

Tucker sucked in a breath then closed the door. His heart raced. *Could she truly be having feelings for him?* He climbed behind the steering wheel and turned on the engine, trying to tell himself to calm down and take this slow. "Just don't overreact. Just take this slow." *Well, that very well might have been a bad thing to say.*

She didn't say anything.

He gave a sideways glance, and she didn't move either. Her expression was not good. They were almost back to the road that would take them to their cabins when she turned toward him.

"I don't see how people overcome this."

It hit him then. "Just because you had a moment when you reacted to me there in the water doesn't mean maybe more than that you're moving forward. Every day is another step forward from the loss you've suffered and to the future that waits for you. My mother knows this all too well. Losing my father was devastating to her. To all of us. But she'd been his, and he'd been hers. I know that to a point with Darla, though we hadn't known each other but almost a year. My mom and dad had loved each other for years and years. You loved Mark for several years, so I'm thinking you might benefit from talking to my mom. When she gets home, she'll be glad to meet you and happy to help you in any way she can. She knows exactly how you're feeling. Maybe a woman and a man feel things differently because I don't think I'm helping at all, just messing things up for you." And that was true.

"I would love to talk to her but not the day she gets home or even the day after. She's starting over and happy. Now is not the time. I'm going to write my book and let these emotions settle down."

He turned onto the county road and headed toward their road. Two miles down the road, he turned and soon pulled behind her car. "Just give me a call if you need me, or if you want to go ahead and go out to see the campgrounds. Or, if you'd rather have Nina go with you, I'm sure she would love to."

She gave him a small smile. "Thank you for understanding. I'll see what tomorrow brings." She opened the door and then gently closed it behind her and, without looking at him, headed toward the cabin.

He watched her go as emotions washed through him. *What was he supposed to do? Back out and go work?* Work had always been his saving grace. Hard work. But first he had to go to the house and get these swim trunks off and put on some work clothes.

CHAPTER THIRTEEN

It was late in the afternoon when Seth carried her over the threshold of his house—their house. Alice smiled at him as they entered the living room, and he kicked the door shut with his foot.

"I love you, Seth and I'm glad to be home in your arms, about to start our life at home and here on Star Gazer Island."

He grinned and kissed her lips. After a moment, he pulled away and hitched his brows. "You and me and new dreams together."

She loved him so much. They were starting their new dream of life together. Not something they'd ever envisioned a few years ago but they didn't control life.

They'd both been blessed once and now twice with their love for each other. "We won't take a moment for granted."

"No, we won't. Now, let's enjoy our first official evening home, and tomorrow we'll celebrate being home with your family out at the ranch dinner Nina and Jackson set up. I'm glad you put off going back to the inn for an extra day. I'm sure they miss you, but you have a wonderful staff. Especially Lisa."

"I'm all in on your idea and you are absolutely right about Lisa. She didn't call me one time while we were on our honeymoon. I cheated and called her one day, and she told me she was so glad we were having a wonderful time and not to worry about the inn; she had it handled. I haven't worried about it since." She cupped his face and kissed him. "You are my focus right now."

She meant it, too. Oh, how she loved this amazing man. She was thankful to have such wonderful help at the inn to give her the time she wanted with him. Life was not to be wasted and they planned to enjoy the work they'd created, enjoy their families but take time to do things together, like travel. But also, time to be grandparents to Landon, Lorna's little boy that they all claimed now and when her kids finally gave her some. She so looked forward to Nina and Jackson having their baby.

But right now, it was her and Seth and as his arms tightened around her, her heart pounded with love.

* * *

Tucker arrived at his brother's house the next evening, after his confusing day with Maggie yesterday. He'd pushed himself to keep his distance and not to call her or stop as he was passing by. Seeing his mother and new stepdad tonight and welcoming them home was a welcomed distraction.

He arrived about the time everyone was, and like his brothers Riley and Dallas were doing, he followed them straight to Seth's truck as it pulled in beside them. Riley reached his mom's door first and pulled it open, and helped her out of the cab and straight into his arms.

"Don't you look great." He hugged her tightly, then pulled back to smile down at her. "And happy and tanned. It's great to see you both looking this happy."

"It's all true. We are, and it's good to get such a wonderful welcome home." She cupped Riley's cheek, then chuckled as Dallas slipped his arm between them and pulled her into his hug.

"My turn. But I agree with Riley. You look great. We are excited to spend the evening with y'all." Dallas kissed the top of their mother's head, then grinned at Tucker. "Okay, Tuck, your turn."

His mother was chuckling as she slipped from Dallas's hug into his. Tucker embraced her tightly, so glad to see her shining with happiness and feeling the spark of positivity for himself. He would not give up on what he was feeling for Maggie; he would be patient like Seth had been to win his mom's love. The looks on their faces told him that it was worth it.

"I'm so glad to see you smiling so big. Welcome home, Mom, and you, too, Seth." He held his hand out to Seth, who grinned.

"Thanks. We're glad to be home to get our life together flowing, but we had a fantastic time on the honeymoon. Now, I'm glad to officially be a part of the family." He looked around at Tucker and his brothers and their wives, who now stood beside them, waiting on hugs.

Tucker released his mom and stepped back as she was welcomed home by the ladies. Then he followed everyone to the back porch, where Jackson and Nina waited for them. They'd refused any help on getting the dinner ready, just a little barbeque and potato salad night meant for eating and talking, and he was sure lots of laughter. They were all thrilled to see their mother happy again and he knew his father was too. This was going to be a great evening.

"How are you feeling?" His mother's first question was to Nina as she hugged her.

"Wonderful. I have some morning sickness but expect that to be better after this next month. I don't mind it though because as long as I'm having a baby, I can take some morning sickness."

Everyone smiled, and he did too. He'd love to have kids one day, but if that never happened, he planned to be the best uncle out there.

"You are going to be a wonderful mother with that

attitude. It will get better. At least mine did." His mom smiled.

"Okay, you ladies can help me finish getting everything out of the ovens and refrigerator, and I don't want to hear anything about how you wanted to help. I know you did, but this was a really easy dinner to get together."

He watched as his two sisters-in-law, Sophie, and his mom entered the house through the glass double doors, all of them talking in response to Nina's words. He grinned as he turned back to his brothers and Seth. "That's going to be an in-depth conversation. I can't believe she didn't let them help."

Jackson laughed. "She is having a little bit of trouble sleeping and moving around helps her, so she just insisted, and I didn't try to talk her out of it. Y'all know the meat is a big deal and the corn on the cob on the grill helps too. But she insisted on doing potato salad instead of me doing baked potatoes on the grill, and right now, my Nina gets whatever she wants." He grinned and Tucker felt his brother's happiness.

"I think that's great," Seth said. "Your mom is

thrilled about the idea of being a grandmother again. I know I'll be filling in for your dad, but know I'm honored I'll get to help raise or play with any kids you all end up having. It wasn't a hope I had until falling for your mother. Y'all and your coming families are a huge asset that I'll always cherish."

"We are just as glad to have you standing in for Dad," Dallas said. "I'm doing that for Landon and loving every moment of it…in my heart he's my son. We're looking forward to having one together but it will mean the same since I love that little boy and his mom with all my heart."

Everyone started talking about how much the kids were all going to mean when they all had them. Tucker had taken a seat and listened to the happiness of the conversation. His thoughts went to Darla and their lost dreams, and then straight to Maggie. *Was his life always going to be like this?*

He focused, pulling his thoughts from Maggie, back to knowing with or without a woman in his life, he was going to love being an uncle to Landon and all the kids his three brothers were going to have. Life was going to be good and after having spent the last several years overcoming his grief, he refused to let himself fall back and grieve what he might not ever have again—the love of a special woman.

He just had to hang onto that thought and not let his mind slide backward into the quicksand of heartache and heartbreak.

* * *

"So, how are wedding plans going, Sophie? You two have been very quiet," Alice said, placing ice in one of the glasses she was filling for everyone. She wanted this sweet woman to say they were going great and it would be soon, but she had no right to let her wishes out. This was Sophie and Riley's choice.

Sophie's eyes twinkled as everyone looked at her. "Y'all will be the first to find out. We aren't exactly to the decision on when but you'll know soon. We were just waiting until you and your sweetie got home from your honeymoon before making our decision."

"Great. I'm sure everyone is with me on being

ready to hear some news." Alice was thrilled at the excitement in Sophie's voice. From the looks on Nina's and Lorna's faces, she had a feeling they were too. *Or did they know more than she did?* She wouldn't press. This was Sophie and Riley's announcement, and she wouldn't take anything away from what they were planning. But she had a funny feeling the information was coming soon and that pleased her so very much.

"I have something to tell all of you," Lorna said from where she was filling ice into cups while she let Alice enjoy time with her son. "Dallas and I are excited because I take a test tomorrow to see if we are expecting a baby. I'm too excited to hide it from all of you, and he knows I'm probably telling you now."

Gasps and sounds of excitement exploded, and Alice's heart throbbed gleefully. "I'm so thrilled. When will you know?"

"Tomorrow morning. If we are, we will be making calls to everyone if we're having a baby."

"That's wonderful." Nina went over to hug Lorna.

Alice got up off the floor, then did the same. "I can't wait for a call."

"Me too." Sophie wrapped her arms around Lorna when Alice released her. "And I can tell you that after Riley and I tie the knot, we aren't waiting long either. Alice, you're going to have all those grandbabies you were dreaming about fairly quickly."

"And I'll welcome them." Alice reached down and picked up little toddling Landon and hugged him close. "You're going to be a big brother, little fella. A very good one." Oh, how she loved this little one her son had also fallen in love with as he fell for the baby's mother. Life was looking so sparkling and wonderful. She walked over to the window and stared out at her sons talking with her husband. Her world was perfect.

Her eyes landed on sweet Tucker, and she saw his eyes as he looked at his happy brothers and new stepfather. Wishful eyes studied them and drank in their words. Alice hoped with every ounce of her being that soon he would experience what she had after the loss of her love. He deserved the happiness they were all feeling, and she hoped it would happen shortly.

"Now," Sophie turned to Nina, "how is your friend who moved into the cabin near Tucker doing? They are supposed to come out to the campsite one day, and I think Riley is excited about it."

Alice was immediately alert. "Who are you talking about?" She'd heard nothing about this, but she'd heard something in Sophie's tone, and especially that Riley was excited. Excited about what—the fact that his brother might be bringing a woman to the camp? She was suddenly excited, too, and had no idea who this was.

Nina's gaze met hers. "You haven't met my friend who moved into the cabin down from Tucker the day you and Seth got married. Maggie is a wonderful lady. She's an author with a great reputation, but she lost her husband about two years ago. She's still overcoming that but trying to get back into writing."

"I'm so sorry about her husband," Alice said as everyone echoed her words. "But was Tucker upset that you put her out there near him? I know he stressed that he wanted to be out there alone."

"He got used to it. I didn't mean anything by it and let him know quickly that she didn't want to be bothered either. That I just couldn't stand putting her way out in one of the cabins with no one around. Just in case she had an emergency. Thankfully, Tucker didn't get too upset and in the end he's helped her on her research of the ranch for book scenes. This is the first book she's written since losing her husband, Mark, in a terrible highway crash."

Sophie looked around. "Riley said he seemed a bit more up in his mood the other day when they met in town, and he invited them out as soon as he heard she was looking for locations for scenes in her book. But mostly he was happy to see what he took as a spark in Tucker's eyes. A spark he's never seen. I think he's hoping something good could be happening."

"Y'all, I never even thought of this when I put her out there. I was only thinking about her aching heart and not wanting her to be out in the boonies late at night without someone near. But maybe, maybe there is hope here. Both of them have lost the loves of their lives—so be aware that nothing could come of this. I'm thinking maybe they can at least help each other."

Alice couldn't speak as she knew exactly everything there was about having the death of a loved one in common. It had helped her and Seth understand each other, and had driven Seth to give her time. "Thank you for letting me know, because I won't be taken by surprise if Tucker says anything. But all of you, from my perspective, I'll tell you not to push. Don't ask him tons of questions because Tucker is a very private man. Especially after losing Darla."

"I second that," Nina said.

"I promise I only brought it up here," Sophie said. "I'd never say anything in front of either of them unless they said something. But I would love to meet her."

"I agree with everyone," Lorna said. "And I would also love to meet her. After such a loss, we wouldn't want her to feel alone."

"Thank you all." Nina smiled at them all. "Now that Alice is home, we're going to have a girl time, maybe lunch at the inn, and I'll make sure she's there. It's a place I think she'll want in her story, or a place with a fake name that's very similar."

Alice loved these ladies and the hearts they all had. "I can't wait. You let me know and I'll be there and set it up."

Everyone agreed.

"Great," Nina said. "Now y'all grab something and let's head out and get this party started."

"I'll bring this handsome little toddling fella with me." Alice reached down for Landon, and he grinned at her and wrapped his arms around her neck. She kissed his cheek. "Come to Grammy," she said, having chosen a name he might take hold of as he was starting to juggle words at last.

"Gammy." He grinned at her.

Everyone chuckled and she let loose an excited chuckle herself. "Whatever you want to call me is perfect. I'll take it."

"I love it, but it could change," Lorna said, adoring eyes on her son. "He started out calling me Mada, I think a combination of Momma and Daddy. That's how Dallas was talking to him about us, as Momma and Daddy, and I think he combined them. So stay tuned for what he eventually calls you."

"I'll love anything he lays on me."

Everyone was smiling as she opened the door and carried Landon out, and they followed. This was going to be a fantastic dinner in more ways than her and Seth's welcome home dinner—which was wonderful. But now, she had hope about more grandbabies and maybe a new love on the horizon for Tucker.

CHAPTER FOURTEEN

"You've been quieter than usual this evening. What's on your mind?"

Tucker looked down at his mother. She'd just come up beside him after their talkative dinner and now everyone was standing around, enjoying the evening. He'd moved to the corner of the patio and stared out across the fenced pool toward the pastures. He took a deep breath and decided now was as good a time as any to talk to her.

"I'm not sure you've heard there is someone staying in the cabin near mine. I figure someone mentioned it to you but nothing was said about it tonight. Not even from Nina, who is her friend."

"Yes, I did hear there was a widow romance writer out there right now. Nina told me and we all talked a little about it, worried it could be putting stress on you."

"No stress. I was thinking it would at first but I understand why Nina put her out there near me, and I'm watching out for her. She needs it, I think. She's still in that time where mourning is really rough. You know, that time when the present starts pressing that it's time to let go some and start living again." He knew that feeling immensely and had finally given in and started living again, but still not completely. "You know where I'm coming from."

She wrapped her arm around his waist and gave him a side hug. "I understand completely. You've had a longer period to make progress. Some people make it fast and for others like us, it doesn't happen the same way. But you and Seth both had nearly seven years to adjust to life and start to hope for more. At least, that was how it was for Seth when we met. I'm thinking you're at that same spot. Not that I'm taking anything for granted with you and your new neighbor. But Nina said it had been about two years since losing her husband, which was about what my loss was of your dad when I met Seth. He was ready when we met, only he hadn't been ready until he met me. Are you by chance feeling anything like that? You look really concerned when you talk about her."

He'd barely said anything, and his mom had picked up on his feelings. "Yes, it came over the first few meetings—but I'm only telling you my feelings, Mom and maybe Seth, if you end up talking to him about it. I don't want to hurt her. Something I said pushed her away the other day."

"Hang in there and give her space, but don't just abandon her. Seth gave me space but he was working at the inn so we couldn't just escape each other. You live down the road from Maggie, and on the ranch she's researching. I have no doubt that you'll see each other and if you are supposed to end up together, being patient might help. She may have feelings for you that she's just having a hard time coming to terms with, like I had to do with my feelings for Seth."

His mom was right. He had to get out of this down mood he was in and back on encouraging, friendly terms with Maggie. What would be would be, when and if it was supposed to be. "Thanks, Mom." He wrapped his arm around her shoulders and gave her a gentle squeeze. "I'm really glad not everyone has to go through the loss that we and Maggie have gone through."

She looked up at him. "I am too. But we each have a time here on earth, and they don't always match so we have to adjust and revive. Sometimes love finds us again. Be ready for when it truly happens to you because I can tell you are ready. I'm also sure your first love is happy for you."

His heart clenched with thoughts of Darla, her loving spirit, and he knew his mother was right.

* * *

Maggie had been writing in the living room and it was around nine o'clock when Tucker's truck passed by, heading to his cabin. She forced herself to stay in the chair and not go out the door and chase him down so that she could apologize to him. It had taken the rest of yesterday and today of struggling with her turbulent emotions, but she knew she couldn't hold her emotions against him. He had done nothing wrong except try to help her with her book settings. The fact that her emotions…and maybe his, too…had tangled was not his fault. It was something that had just happened, and she had to come to terms with it. But it could wait until the daylight hours. So, she closed her computer and stood. It was time to get ready for bed.

Her phone rang as she entered her bedroom and laid her phone on the bedside table. She glanced down at the phone and saw it was Nina. She quickly picked it up. "Hi, is everything okay?" Her pregnant friend didn't normally call this late.

"Yes, it's fine. Jackson's mom and stepdad made it home, and we had dinner together here at our house. It was great, and I told her about you. She really wants to meet you, as do my sister-in-law and soon-to-be sister-in-law. So I told them I'd call you and see if you want to have lunch at the inn tomorrow with everyone—not the guys, just us gals. You've been holed up for a few days and I think it would be a good thing. You wanted to see the inn."

Maggie didn't miss how much her friend was pushing this, as if she expected her to back away. "I would love to. I want to meet them all also."

"Great. Then I'll come by and pick you up a little before eleven, if that's okay. We think it would be a little less crowded early rather than wait until noon. The restaurant draws tourists but also regulars on lunch break. It's just a lovely place with delicious food."

Excitement that she needed filled Maggie. "I'm all in. Thanks for the invite."

"Wonderful. See you in the morning."

Maggie stared at the phone for a second after hanging up, then she smiled and set it back on the bedside table. Tomorrow was going to be a great day and she couldn't wait.

By morning, she jumped from bed and had her coffee out at the outside table. She could see from where she sat that Tucker had already left for the day. He must have left earlier than usual this morning. She would go to his cabin this evening if she had to, to apologize to him. But right now she had a cup of coffee to drink, then a shower and maybe a few words written before she and

Nina headed to meet his family at the inn. She couldn't wait to meet everyone and to see the inn. She was also going to meet his mother, someone she wanted to meet very much.

By the time Nina picked her up and they were heading into town, she was even happier her friend had set up the lunch date. "I can't wait to meet everyone."

"Oh, believe me, they all said last night at the dinner that they wanted to meet you, so we decided to see if you wanted to meet today. It was meant to be. You will love the inn, it's just beautiful and for Alice, it's the place she fell in love with the boys' dad and the place she fell in love with her sweet new husband. It's a wonderful, magical place. I love every time Jackson and I go there because it's also where I met him."

"That belongs in a love story," Maggie said, and meant it.

"I agree. I think everyone's love story means just as much to them. I'm sure you have plenty of plots to come up with in that creative mind of yours."

She looked at her friend. "I do. I don't really use anyone's real love story. I come up with characters first and then let their own story develop. So, as much as I love your story, I wouldn't trample on it by putting it in a book. *But,* I might steal a location and put them in the same place, like the lake that Tucker took me to. He said Jackson took you there. It's a wonderful place."

Nina smiled at her, love dancing in her eyes. "It is. You saw my picture, so you know how much we love it."

"I totally understand after seeing the beautiful place and swimming in it, so I am using it." Her mind lurched suddenly as she thought of Tucker and the emotions she felt when they were there in that water. Emotions she was still trying to understand but not be mad about.

"You went swimming there? Please tell me Tucker went with you and that you didn't go alone. It's too far out in the boonies to go alone."

"He went with me. Believe me, he was watching out for me."

"Fantastic. He's a really good guy, and I'm glad he's helping you out."

"Yes, he is and very good at giving me suggestions and then giving me time to write, and for me to be the one to contact him if I want to go exploring. One of the places I'm going to get him to take me is the campground."

Nina pulled into the inn's parking lot. "You will love it. You're going to love Riley's fiancée too. I think they are getting ready to surprise us with a wedding date. We are all waiting to hear what's up their sleeves. They wouldn't announce anything until his mom and Seth's wedding and honeymoon were over, wanting to give them the spotlight. But now we are all waiting impatiently for an announcement."

"That's interesting. I know you're excited."

"Totally. Now, let's go have a wonderful lunch with everyone. They are all eager to meet you. Some even love to read and have your books on their bookshelf."

They entered through the front door though there was a second entrance straight to the restaurant that Nina told her had been added not too long ago. But most people liked to enter through the inn's entrance and get the feel of the pretty inn and to say hello to Alice if she was working the front desk.

As soon as they entered the front room, Maggie's gaze swept around, taking in the stairway leading upstairs, the pretty chairs near the window, the tall reception desk that sat at the edge of the entrance room, and a hallway that she could see led to the back of the house. Glass doors could be seen there she could see was the restaurant entrance from here. There were pretty paintings on the wall; gorgeous water paintings and some beautiful water bird paintings led the way up the stairs.

"Did you paint all these?" she asked Nina.

"The big ones. I'm more of waterscapes and landscapes than I am these beautiful bird portraits. I love them but didn't paint them. Alice has great taste in decorating and they fit beautifully."

"Just the entrance is wonderful, and I can't wait to see the rest."

"I'll be thrilled to show you," said a beautiful older woman who came from the door into the restaurant. "I'm Alice, this sweet, beautiful Nina's mother-in-law. You, I assume, are Maggie."

Maggie was taken over by the happiness that swam around the lady. "Yes, and I'm so glad to meet you.

Congratulations on your marriage, Nina told me he's a wonderful man."

"Yes, he is. Love is sometimes unexpected, and he was to me. I never believed I'd fall in love again after being so in love with the boys' dad. But I did and I'm thrilled. I'm so sorry you lost your husband, your love. But I'm glad you are here and starting back to writing again and finding your new path in life, which you have to do. Your sweet husband will always live in your heart but moving forward is necessary. I did that with opening this inn. Did Nina tell you that?"

"Yes, and I'm glad to meet you. I'm struggling to get my feet back on the ground without Mark but I'm determined to do it. I can feel him urging me on." And she meant it.

Nina and Alice both smiled gently at her.

Alice spoke as she slipped her arm through hers. "I'm sure he is doing just that. I know my William was doing that for me and, like you are doing, I was pushing myself to find a new life. I believed it was reopening this inn that was meant to be and now I love my inn. It led me to my new love as it did to my first love, so it's special to my heart. Now, let's go join the others, who are very excited to meet you. They all ordered some of your books online and can't wait to get them and become fans. I'm doing the same thing."

Her heart melted at that. "You all don't have to do that. I will like you whether you're a fan or not."

Alice patted her arm as Nina held the door to the restaurant open for them. "We are more than excited to meet you as a person and the books just add to the excitement. So don't worry that your books are the only reason we're glad to meet you."

She smiled. "I have a feeling this is going to be a great day. To be honest, seeing you so happy makes me delighted and hopeful."

"Great," Alice said as she led the way through the pretty dining area then out onto the deck. Each table had a teal-toned umbrella, giving the tables a good space between them and making it very colorful.

She spotted two women sitting at a table at the iron fence that separated the dining area from the garden and trails a few steps below the dining area. They were watching them approach with smiles on their faces and they stood up as she, Nina, and Alice reached them.

"Ladies, this is the sweet Maggie Carson. Maggie,

this is Lorna, who is married to my son Dallas and this is Sophie, who is engaged to my son Riley."

Both of the pretty ladies reached out for her hand and grasped it together as they smiled at her.

"We are so glad to meet you," Sophie said. "I hope you're enjoying your stay at the ranch."

"I agree with Sophie," Lorna said. "I really hope you're enjoying yourself, and that being out here is helpful to you. We are all so sorry for your loss and just want you to know that."

They squeezed her hand then let go as she took a breath, touched by their kindness. "Thank you all. When Nina asked me to come out and try to get back to writing, I thought about it then grabbed hold of the idea because I needed a change. I'm so glad I came."

Nina stepped in and hugged her. "Me too. Now let's all sit down and get comfortable."

Everyone moved around the table, pulling out their chairs and taking a seat. They were a happy group and so welcoming. Maggie was more than thrilled that she was here. Just as they sat, a very lovely older lady, somewhere in the age range of Alice, maybe a bit younger, walked out the dining room door. She wore what looked like chef clothing—black pants and a white shirt—and she was immediately met with comments from all the tables about how delicious the food was. She smiled and thanked everyone as she came to their table.

Alice smiled up at her, then at Maggie. "This is my good friend and head chef, Lisa Blair. Lisa, this is Maggie Carson, who is staying at the ranch in one of the cabins."

Lisa held out her hand. "I'm glad to meet you. I know you're going to enjoy your stay. The ranch is wonderful, but the town is too. I've loved every moment here since moving over from Corpus Christi. I'm in the little red house right past the inn, it is wonderful. Nina lived there before she married Jackson."

Maggie looked in the direction Lisa nodded and could barely see over the wall and pretty bushes the red of the house. She smiled. "I'm sure it's great being on the water and so close to your work."

"Yes, it is. I'm loving it. This is a wonderful place to start over, and I'm very glad I found it—the house, the inn, and all of these lovely ladies you are hanging out with today. So, I just wanted to come out and welcome all of you here for lunch."

Everyone talked at once, smiling and assuring Lisa that they were glad to be here and that they couldn't, as always, wait to get her special food. Maggie loved it all—watching them, seeing the adoration and friendship flowing between them. She wanted this.

The idea that had tugged at her early on when arriving at the ranch tugged harder: *I could move here. Start over. Begin again.*

She knew right then and there that she was going to talk to Nina about this. She knew that somehow Lisa had understood she might need it. She wondered what her story was and knew she would ask Nina about that too.

After Lisa left to get back to cooking and a waitress took their drink orders, they all opened their menus.

"This is the lunch menu," Alice said. "The dinner menu has different options, so you'll have to come back and let me treat you to dinner sometime."

Her gaze scanned the menu: salads, soups, homemade bread and then warm sandwiches, and usual dining beside the sea options like shrimp and wonderful-sounding fish and vegetables. She looked at Alice, who smiled at her. "This looks wonderful. I'm sure I'll be back to test out the evening menu too, but I might have to start eating lunch here every day." She laughed but meant every word.

"I know the feeling," Lorna said. "I, too, would eat here every day."

"Me too," was echoed from everyone else.

Alice chuckled. "If you all did, then I would get to see you every day. I wouldn't get to eat with you every day but just your smiling faces are wonderful. Speaking of you, Lorna, where is that adorable little boy today?"

Lorna's smile that spread across her face was delightful. "He's with his daddy. Y'all should have seen his excitement when I lifted him up to ride in the saddle with Dallas. They were just going to check some fence lines, not work cattle or anything like that, so he's safely enjoying his time with his daddy. As is his dad enjoying himself."

Everyone was now focused on Lorna and she realized it, looking from one to the other. Maggie knew something was in the air just from their expectant looks.

Lorna chuckled. "Okay, okay, I didn't want to take anything away from meeting Maggie but I can tell what you are all asking and yes, this morning I did the pregnancy test while Dallas paced the kitchen, waiting…we're having a baby."

Maggie, sitting beside her, laid her hand on this lovely lady's hand and squeezed. "So wonderful. Congratulations."

"Thank you," Lorna said, but her reply was drowned out by all the family's squeals of happiness and congratulations.

It was obvious that everyone had been waiting with anticipation for her results. Maggie's heart raced. She had been ready for a baby when Mark had been killed. Now, she might never have a baby unless she could move forward. Some women, she knew, raised children on their own but she wasn't in that space either. She had to move forward. She had to, and she knew Mark would want her to.

Alice lifted her glass of tea and everyone around the table did, too. "We are so happy and ready to welcome another baby to the group." Everyone leaned their glasses in and touched Lorna's. "Just think…next year I'll have three grandbabies—and will welcome more announcements, if they are coming."

Everyone chuckled at that as they took a sip of their drinks.

Sophie grinned, looking somewhat secretive. "I have to get married before I let myself fulfill my dream of babies. So I do hope you are all prepared for our secret announcement that's coming soon."

That was a strange sort of announcement, Maggie thought. The answer, "We're ready," swept around the table. *What was up?* She was startled when Sophie looked at her with dancing eyes.

"When we make an announcement, you are also invited. I have a great feeling you and all of us are going to be great friends."

"Thank you. I'm loving this. I've been so lost in grief the last two years that today has just been a huge bright light of joy, and I'm so thrilled to be here."

And she was. Yes, sadness for her loss of her love would always be with her, but the light of hope shining on the horizon told her that her life could be happy again. With her love of Mark still in her heart but where a new life now grew. Like a mark of one life so loved and a new mark of the new life before her. Hope filled her heart and the desire to find that new life and embrace it sent even more hope flowing through her.

CHAPTER FIFTEEN

Tucker had forced himself to pass by Maggie's cabin again and he'd gotten home, taken a shower, and put on non-starched jeans he liked to relax in and a pale-blue T-shirt. He sat on the bed and pulled on a pair of leather comfort shoes he wore when he was at home. He'd learned he was going to be an uncle again today from a call from Dallas, and he'd told him Lorna was announcing it to all the ladies at lunch, so he was calling all his brothers.

Tucker was thrilled. Another nephew or niece. This was exciting for both Dallas and Jackson, and he was happy for them. He stood and headed into the kitchen alone. *Alone* echoed through him. His brothers were moving along, and it was starting to slam into him.

A knock on his door sounded. He halted, startled because a visitor out here was few and far between, which was exactly why he originally chose this cabin. Lately, it had been growing not so welcomed.

Who was here?

He strode to the front door and pulled it open and froze seeing the beautiful Maggie standing before him, holding a casserole dish. "Maggie, hello." She had a serious look on her face as she watched him, and his heart thundered.

"I'm here to apologize for my behavior the other day. I'm so sorry I treated you so bad."

"I understood. I've been in your shoes. But I'm glad you're here, speaking to me again." He pulled the door open. "Please come in. What did you bring?" He fought to make his voice level as he took in her words, her appearance, and the fact that she was walking across his threshold. Then she smiled at him, and his world lit up with hope. He was so in trouble.

"It's homemade chicken enchiladas. I hope you like them."

"They're homemade by you, so I'm sure I'm going to love them. But only if you're staying to share them with me."

She smiled at him and walked toward the kitchen, which was visible from the entrance. "Thank you for the invitation. I believe I'll join you."

Tucker chuckled. "You've made my day. If you want some, I have chips and dip I can add to the mix, and fresh-made tea."

Maggie set the casserole on the stovetop and turned toward him. "I'm all in."

They stared at each other, and he had to fight off the desire to take her into his arms and feel her against him. It was an overwhelming need that almost made his knees weak. But he was not running her off again. "It's not too hot out on my deck. Would you want to eat out there?"

"Sounds perfect."

Yes, it did, with her here beside him. *Tone this excitement down, Mister Mistake Maker.* The words raced through him, and he forced his excitement down. "Okay, so let's get it all together and head that way. That smells delicious."

Moments later, they had warmed cheese dip from a bought bottle sitting on the patio table beside the nacho chips he'd placed in a large bowl, and the casserole now had its foil off the top and looked delicious. It smelled even better, and his stomach growled.

"I love that it's making your stomach growl like that." She grinned cutely.

"Then it can growl some more if it makes you love—it." He paused, having almost messed up by saying *if it makes you love me*. What a goof up that would have been. He pulled out her chair and she sank into it. He did the same with his that was across from her, farther away than he'd like it to be, and it had him thinking about getting a small table out here. One for two instead of for four.

"I heard today at lunch with all the ladies in your family that you're going to be an uncle again. Two coming this year, plus Lorna's little boy. I haven't met him yet, but everyone was talking about what a cute little fella he was and how happy they were. Are you excited about more babies to be an uncle to?"

"I love it. I'm planning on being the best uncle out there." Tucker didn't say more because he couldn't chance saying anything about how aware it made him of maybe never being the daddy he'd wanted to be.

They each filled their plates and then their gazes locked. Unable to help himself, he placed his hand palm up onto the table for her. "I need to say a blessing. This really is."

Maggie hesitated then slipped her fingers into his, and he wrapped his around them. Joy, thick and true, filled him as he bowed his head and said a quick, heartfelt thank-you for the food and Maggie's friendship. He finished the prayer, though he was tempted to pray all night if it meant he could continue to hold her hand. But he released it because he knew that wasn't possible without maybe running her away again.

"I'm so glad I came to apologize." She reached for her fork.

"You didn't have to apologize, but I'm glad you made the first move to come see me. I've been fighting off wanting to stop and see how you were doing because I know you were working. Honestly, I was worried about you."

She was about to take a bite and paused. "I'm sorry I caused you to worry. After dinner, I'd like to talk about something but not over dinner. Everything is fine, though."

His curiosity was up and he wanted to talk now but nodded. "Whenever you want to talk, I'm here."

Her lips lifted. "Thanks. Now I just want you to enjoy the meal I made you."

"No problem with doing that. It's amazing. Where did you learn to cook like this?"

"My wonderful mother. She was an awesome cook. My dad left us when I was about two. She took a job as a cook in a small-town café and it became a draw for people, similar to what I believe is going on at your mother's inn. That food at the inn was amazing and no wonder since Lisa, the chef, looked like she loved what she did. My mother did too. So, I helped in the kitchen growing up and learned to cook. Then I helped out when I was old enough but I knew it wasn't what I always wanted to do. I loved to read, and after my high school senior year, I sat down and tried writing a romance. It was an experience and I was hooked immediatly. It took me a little while to sell my first book, but now I'm published and I'm so grateful to all those who found my books and loved them. My mother was a great supporter of me, too, and very excited I found something that made me happy."

"Me too. Does she still work at the restaurant?"

"No, she finally remarried and Archie loves her dearly. They are touring the country right now in a motor home. They put it off after Mark died, but I was very quick to let them know that I needed time alone and that I didn't resent them going off and enjoying themselves. So, finally they did just that, and even though their hearts hurt for me, they are having a wonderful time."

"That's great. My family knew after what I went through losing Darla that I didn't want them hovering over me, and I didn't want to talk about it, so they pulled back and gave me space. I threw myself into my ranch work and slowly found my life again. I'm hoping you do the same. This is a great place to do that."

She'd taken a bite but even though she was chewing, she smiled a closed-mouth smile. Then, when she was done, she wiped her mouth and set her fork down. The silence of the night suddenly seemed to surround them as she took a breath and entwined her fingers as if to keep them still.

"That's part of my reason for being here. I think I want to move here. I love the area and all the women in your family have been so welcoming and have made me feel so good. Your sweet mother, too. As mixed up and emotional as I was that day at the lake with you, I also know I'm healing here." She paused, her expression tense. "Tucker, as much as it scares me, I want to get to know you better. *If* you feel the same way, but if not, I understand. I can't promise anything but I also can't deny that there is something between us. Do you agree?"

His heart had busted out of his chest and was somewhere racing around the sun as he looked into her emotional eyes. "Yes," he blurted, unable to hide the happiness her words had ejected him into. "I think you're going to love living here, and I know I'm going to love it and so will my family. But, the fact that you're willing to give me a try with these feelings that have overcome me since meeting you is all I can ask. A chance is better than a closed door and if nothing happens from it, I'll still be happy you're here." He prayed something good would happen between them. He knew from his side of the story that he was already there, where love and wanting a future with her existed. Unable to not do it, he reached for her hand, and she slipped hers into it. "I don't want to put pressure on you but I'm happy." So much more than happy, but he held back.

"I'm not sure what to do now, but…could you hug me?"

He nearly knocked his chair over, standing up. His heart thundered against his ribs. "I would love to. If you're sure."

She stood and nodded. "Please. This is my first step forward and, Tucker, I know Mark is rooting me on."

That was all he needed. He slipped his arms gently around her and stepped close, hugging her against his chest and relishing the feel of her against him. Then she laid her head on his chest and her arms around him tightened. Her heart thundered and he hoped it was for feelings for him and not regret for her husband. His heart ached for the man who'd been so lucky. He'd felt lucky for having had Darla in his life, but this was a new life and he wanted this beautiful, loyal wonderful woman as his own. If only she could let him in.

"Are you okay?" he asked gently, feeling her tremble.

"Better than I've been in a very, very long time." She looked up at him, and he was drawn to her.

His lips were almost to hers when he stopped himself. He didn't want to rush her. This was his chance and he couldn't mess it up.

* * *

Every cell of her being shook as Maggie prepared for Tucker's lips on hers. Anticipation and longing swirled in her, so much that all other thoughts disappeared. She stretched on her toes to reach his lips and welcome them as a need so strong overtook her.

And then he paused. "Do you want this?" he asked softly, though his voice was rough with what she thought was emotion.

Touched by his pausing, she lifted the last small space between them and kissed him. Drank in his lips as his arms tightened around her and his lips took over hers. Her heart pounded as she clung to him and emotions she hadn't felt since losing Mark raged to overtake her. Then, he pulled away and looked down into her eyes. Her breath was hard, her emotions wild.

"That is powerful. Are you all right?" Concern filled his expression.

She nodded and though breathing out of control, she answered, "I'm good. Crazy out of control but good. I need to get my heart calmed down."

He smiled and, taking her hand, he led her over to the swing that sat at the edge of the patio near the empty firepit. Her blood raged as if a fire was burning on this summer night. He sat down first then tugged her hand, and she sank down beside him.

"That was a dream come true for me," he said gently. "But I know we need to take it slow, so I'm sorry if I got carried away."

"No, I got carried away. I couldn't help myself."

He smiled at her. "That brings me joy. But is this the first time since you lost Mark that you've kissed someone?"

"Yes. I haven't even felt a slight urge before, but with you it felt right."

His expression softened and his eyes brightened as they dug deep into hers. "That makes my day, my everything, but I also know how much you love your husband—even gone—and I don't want to do anything to hurt you. It worries me."

She looked out into the dark night and could feel his eyes still on her face. His words showed her how much he understood losing a very much loved one. But she also knew she wanted to move forward and Mark was urging her on. She turned toward Tucker on the swing…the loveseat.

"I don't want to hurt you in case this isn't what I can handle, but I feel so drawn to you. I want to spend time with you and get to know you more. So it's up to you if you want to continue our friendship and this relationship I feel growing between us." *Would he say yes?* The question banged through her with hard stampeding beats as his hands on her tightened and a smile grew across his face that had her heart thundering even harder with happy anticipation.

"I'm your friend, and I want more than anything else in the world to build a personal relationship with you. I haven't wanted more in a relationship since I lost Darla but with you…I'm already falling in love with you. Not that you need to let that put any kind of pressure on you, but I'm just being honest with you."

Her stomach clinched and her breath caught at his words. But instead of turning and running away, she leaned forward and placed her lips to his. She felt him smile against her lips, then his arms went around her and tugged her close as he deepened the kiss. Her life had a huge flash of sunlight and she felt as if they stood inside a rainbow.

CHAPTER SIXTEEN

"Last night I kissed her, and then she kissed me," Tucker said in his office the next morning when Jackson came looking for him because he hadn't met him and his brothers for coffee in the other barn.

"That's wonderful. Sounds like it made you happy. Did it make her happy?"

Tucker raked a hand through his short hair. "It seemed like it. She wants to try a relationship with me and that makes me nearly explode with happiness and fear. What if she realizes some time into the relationship that she made a mistake? I'll get left hanging with my love dangling and mourning again."

His brother reached out and gripped his shoulder.

"Do you believe she is worth the risk? Worth the fight to win her love if you need to?"

The words slammed into him like a steel rod being swung by a mass of men. He knew that already he loved her and would do everything to win her love. If it wasn't meant to be, he loved her enough to walk away. "Yes. I'll fight for her and then let her go, if that's what it takes."

Jackson smiled. "Then you have your answer and my blessing and prayers. You are a great man, and I'm proud to call you my brother. I want you to have the joy that I and your other brothers have."

Tucker took the words in and then, looking at the depth of hope in Jackson's expression and the hope and determination in his own heart, he smiled. "Then I'm in and willing to swim hard against the waves and whirling waters that may happen. I love her, Jackson. I want the best for her, and I'm hoping I'm part of that. I know she's the best for me."

They both smiled, then Jackson stepped back toward the door. "This is going to be exciting. Now, take her on a date or something. Get this romance started."

He turned and headed out the door, a grin still on his lips.

And leaving Tucker with hope rolling through him.

* * *

"You and Tucker are a couple now?" Nina said. She was at the cabin, had driven here the moment Maggie had called and said she needed to talk to her but didn't want to come to the main house. Now she understood why—she needed to talk but didn't want Tucker to think she was having this discussion with her. Nina was ecstatic. "I'm thrilled. The more I've thought about it, the more I believe this was meant to be."

"But what if I lead him on and then can't go through the strong emotions that I'm feeling for him?" Worry filled Maggie's eyes.

"Stop worrying. Both of you have a loved one rooting for you from the other side. *Also* friends here who want you both to find happiness. Together would be wonderful, but don't feel pressure from any of us as everyone learns of the budding relationship. I can tell you it will be well received, and you'll have everyone rooting for you both, but in the end, it will be up to what your heart can do." Nina hoped with all her heart she'd made sense with her words as Maggie's expression went from worry to what Nina thought was relief.

"Thank you. It feels right. I just need to go with the flow, as Mark used to often say." She smiled. "I can hear him saying it right now, and I'm going to do exactly that."

Nina reached out and hugged her sweet, dear friend. "I love you, girlfriend, and I'm so happy for you. I always believed Mark was an amazing man—always was and still is."

Maggie nodded against her shoulder, squeezed her tight, then stepped away, her lips curling up on the edges. "Yes, he was...I have a feeling Tucker is amazing in some of the same ways and also in his own different ways. I'm looking forward to getting to know him more and more."

"Fantastic! So what's next?"

"Dinner tonight somewhere down the road in a small town with tables that are over the water along a stairway from the restaurant."

"Awesome. That smart man—that is a wonderful restaurant for lunch and dinner. We all love it and I'm sure he knows it would be a wonderful place for a scene in your book."

Nina was so happy and then suddenly her baby kicked her in the stomach for the first time. She gasped as her hand went to the spot and a smile of joy filled her face. "My baby moved for the first time. Here, feel. Goodness, this is wonderful." She reached for Maggie's hand and pressed it against the small pounding the baby was doing. "It's as if he's rooting you on too."

Maggie's smile was enormous, and her eyes glistened with tears. "This is so amazing. You, my dear, sweet friend, are so very blessed."

"Yes, I agree. I must go find Jackson and see if the baby keeps this up. But, Maggie, I'm so glad you got to experience this with me."

"I am too. Drive careful."

Nina was already on the way to the door. "Nothing will make me drive crazy. I'll go slow and directly to the house because he's working on reports today in his office. Have fun tonight."

Maggie walked her to the car and opened the door for her. "I will. You have fun letting your sweet husband in on this gift."

Nina cranked the engine and winked as Maggie closed the door. "I will. Between your wonderful news and my baby showing his spirit, this is a perfect day." Nina fastened her seat belt; then, with a wave, she backed out and headed to share the fun, good news with her husband.

* * *

Tucker's heart was on a jazzy beat as he waited for Maggie to open the door and head to the truck and the date begin. It turned into a firecracker rocket when she opened the door. She wore a pretty, soft-looking lavender dress with low-heeled sand-colored sandals.

"You look stunning." It was the absolute truth.

"Thank you. I'm glad I brought some dressier things along just in case Nina and I did anything that needed something a little dressier than my jeans and T-shirts. I never dreamed I'd be wearing it on a date." A smile eased across her beautiful face.

"I'm glad to help change that thought." He crooked his arm and turned it toward her. "Ready?"

She tucked her arm in his. "Ready." She pulled the door closed, then they headed down the step and he had her in the truck within seconds.

He fought off the desire to pull her into his arms and continue the kissing they'd started last night. No way was he going to run her off by acting too quickly; he knew he needed to take his time. They talked about her having told Nina about them, and he confessed that he had also told Jackson. Then they both laughed and it felt so good.

"Did you talk to Jackson after Nina got back home around noon?"

"No, he was busy in his home office. Why?"

"Because the baby kicked for the first time during our conversation. It was so wonderful to see the awe and joy on Nina's face. I got to feel it also and nearly started crying, it touched me so strongly. She headed home to let Jackson in on the surprise. It was so beautiful to witness."

"I know my brother had a great afternoon then.

He's going to be a great dad and Nina is going to be an amazing mother, I can feel it."

"I agree."

He turned the truck onto the road and headed away from the ranch and toward the place his brothers enjoyed for dates with their wives, or in Riley's case, his soon-to-be wife. He was so happy to have someone to share this place with. They talked some more as he drove, and soon as the sun was coming down, they were led down the stairs along the hill overlooking the river to a table with small hanging lights stretched over the area their table sat. There were more tables above them and below, making this as unique of a place as everyone had said. Along the river, soft spotlights gave them a view of the flowing water.

"This is *amazing*. Thank you for bringing me," Maggie said, her voice in awe.

He grinned, loving her reaction. "I agree. My brothers have had great things to say about it but I've never come until now. Didn't have a reason…I'm glad I'm sharing it with you for the first time."

"Me too." Her gaze reached inside of him, tugging

at his heart before she quickly looked back out to the flowing river.

They ordered their drinks then enjoyed watching the water flow in the lights. Soft music played from the patio above them, where many others were enjoying their meal. Not everyone wanted to walk downstairs on the side of a small cliff overhanging the river, but she and Tucker had done it and loved it. They ordered their meal; then Tucker smiled at her and held his hand out on top of the table. She slipped hers into his, and he wrapped his fingers gently around hers. They enjoyed the music, the scenery, and being together.

"Are you all right?" Tucker brushed his finger across Maggie's in a gentle caress after seeing a flash of emotion in her eyes.

"Yes. Actually, I'm feeling alive. It's something I never expected to feel again."

"I know. I feel the same way. You sparkled up my life with your entrance. I had found my place at the ranch and believed that's how it would be. I knew my mom and brothers were all hoping more would come, but I had decided not to try. Then I found you standing on the counter in the cabin next to me and things began to change. Life has strange ways of introducing people to each other." He grinned and she chuckled, the sound causing his grin to grow.

"You were my hero that night."

He lifted her hand, leaned forward, and kissed her knuckles. "I'm glad, because finding you on top of that kitchen counter will always be remembered as one of the greatest moments in my life." He kissed her knuckles again and watched the tender smile appear on her beautiful face. Yes, he loved her and always would.

The waitress appeared with a tray holding their food. Perfect timing, or he might have stood and pulled her into his arms right there for all to see as he kissed her.

Again, he could not rush this, but he was all in.

CHAPTER SEVENTEEN

"Are you ready?" Riley asked his beautiful fiancée, whom he was so very ready to make his wife.

Sophie's eyes twinkled with merriment as she placed her hand on his wrist. "I'm so very ready. Let's make our calls."

All of his family's numbers were lined up on his phone. "Okay, darlin'. Mom first." He pushed the Call button and the rings sounded as they waited for her to answer.

"Hello, Riley. How are you?"

He grinned at Sophie. "I'm fine. Sophie is here on the phone with me, and we have an invitation for you."

"An invitation to what?" Excitement lit her voice.

"Our wedding." Sophie smiled at him.

"Wedding! I was hoping you'd say that. But if you're just now calling everyone, have you just decided to do it and not invite a lot of people? I am a little confused but happy for you just the same."

Riley chuckled. "Mom, we've been planning this surprise for a little while. We just wanted to announce it and then get on with our life together. Sophie and I both just want our family at the camp where we met to celebrate with us tomorrow."

"You are all my family now. So, though we loved your wedding, we just want our family on the beach where we had our first kiss and knew our world had changed." She smiled at him, and Riley leaned forward and kissed her lightly on the lips.

"I'll be there tomorrow with Seth on my arm and my heart so happy to watch this beautiful event. It will be wonderful. Can I please bring something?"

"No, ma'am. We have it all figured out. Just bring your sweetheart and join us."

"I can't wait. I love you two, and so does Seth. He'll

be excited when I call him."

"We love y'all too," they said together, then ended the call and hugged.

"First one down. Now, we better get busy before Mom calls everyone and asks if we've called."

Sophie chuckled. "Dial that phone."

And he did, calling Dallas, who was over-the-moon excited for them and couldn't wait to tell Lorna. As was Jackson and Nina, who took the call together.

Then he called Tucker, and with a bit more excitement, he exploded with happiness. "I am so glad this is happening at last! Congratulations, you two. So, are you going on a honeymoon?"

"We are going away for that night and the next, and then will be back in time to have the new camp group come in. It's Sophie's camping group, so we want to get back and share the news with them. We'll go on a longer honeymoon later in the year and get you to help then if we need you."

"Sounds good. You both know I'm glad to help out."

"We know, but this is her group, and they were how

we met, so we want to include them in the celebration."

"They are like my family," Sophie added. "We'll be having our dancing and celebrating each evening like before when they came and you helped. Maybe Maggie would want to come. You could also bring her to the wedding if you two are getting along again and she would like to come."

Tucker chuckled. "I was going to ask you if she could be my date."

"Your actual date?" Sophie asked, excitement in her voice. "Does this mean you're actually dating now?"

"Yes. We are. Honestly, I'm hoping it works its way into something lasting. Something happy like you two, and Jackson and Nina, Dallas and Lorna, and Mom and Seth."

Riley grinned so big at his brother's words. "We are rooting for you. Can't wait to see you two together."

"Thanks. See you tomorrow evening with Maggie on my arm."

As soon as Riley disconnected the call, Sophie shot out of her chair and he rose to catch her as she flung her arms around his neck. "I'm so excited for Tucker and for Maggie, they are perfect for each other. This will be so amazing."

He grinned at her and spun her around, lifting her feet from the ground. "I'm thrilled and hopeful for them. But nothing can overpower my love and excitement of marrying you tomorrow night." He stopped turning and kissed her. This was what he now lived for. He loved this woman so much he couldn't even imagine what his brother had gone through, losing his love, or what Maggie had gone through losing her husband, her love. He prayed as he stared into Sophie's eyes that they would live life together to an old and wonderful age.

* * *

Utter excitement hung in the air around Alice as she walked from the lobby of the inn to the restaurant, looking for Lisa. She found her in the kitchen in her usual spot at the grill. It was apparent at Lisa's sudden smile when she looked up and saw her approaching that she had happiness written all over her face.

"What's up? You look ecstatic."

"Finally, Riley and Sophie have announced they are getting married."

"Wonderful! When? And are we doing the wedding?"

Alice chuckled, she was so happy. "No, they are having a private wedding tomorrow night at the camp, with only the family. They already have everything lined up and we are just supposed to show up. Those two just tickle me. They put off announcing it until after Seth and I got married and had our honeymoon. But they are certain this is how they want it so I'm happy for them. They are going away for a couple of nights and then coming back and hosting the camping group Sophie is the leader of and will celebrate with them too. Then later they'll take a real honeymoon."

"That really makes me smile. They are so right for each other."

"Who is right for each other?" Zane asked as he walked up. "If it's none of my business, just ignore me." He grinned as he set the tray of steaks on the counter.

Alice smiled warmly at him, and then shifted her

gaze to her friend and caught the look of longing in Lisa's eyes. It was only there for a second before she hid it and met Alice's gaze. "My son Riley and his fiancée, the beautiful and wonderful Sophie, are having a surprise wedding at their campground tomorrow night for just the immediate family. I love it."

Grinning, the handsome chef nodded. "That's great. I know Seth is going to be happy about it too."

"Yes, he will be. He's in a meeting on a new building project right now, so he doesn't know, but he will be thrilled for them. Don't let me make you two get behind on your cooking, but I had to share."

"I'm glad you did." Lisa had been turning the chicken she was grilling and looked up, her gaze shifted first to Zane.

Again, Alice didn't miss the longing that flickered momentarily in Lisa's gaze once more. This was wonderfully interesting, and Alice hoped there was more to come between these two amazing people.

She turned and headed out, saying hello to the others in the kitchen helping prepare food. They were all too far away from the grill to have heard her announcement, but she didn't pause to tell them. She had a call to Seth to make now that his meeting was probably finished. She loved to talk to him any time of the day but this was super special and she was so happy.

And blessed in so many ways.

CHAPTER EIGHTEEN

Maggie sat at her kitchen table, typing with what felt like the speed of light as the story exploded in her mind. She was alive again. She knew that as much as she'd desperately loved Mark and missed him so much, she had finally started moving forward like she needed to. She also knew much of that was because of Tucker.

A familiar knock on the door had her nearly jumping to her feet. Was Tucker stopping by to say hello? She hurried to the door and swung it open, her hope instantly fulfilled by the smiling cowboy on her porch.

"Tucker, what a nice surprise."

"Glad you think so. Because I think you're a nice view and I'm glad to be here." He grinned. "Can I come in? I have something to ask you."

Something to ask her? Her heart skipped beats. *What was he going to ask her?* "Yes, please." She backed up and he came into the cabin. She closed the door and instantly he took her in his arms and his lips dropped to hers for a soft, warm kiss that sent shivers of anticipation flowing through her.

"Okay, sorry, told myself not to do that but couldn't help it." He gently let her go, and she tried not to stumble as she stepped back, heart racing and lips tingling.

"Riley and Sophie are getting married and just announced the small wedding will be at the camp tomorrow night and is only for family. But a single man, me, can bring a date so I'm asking you. Also, they mentioned you, just in case it could help your writing and because my brothers really want to meet you. So, will you be my date? It's only family there other than you but believe me when I say they are all hoping you will come."

A smile burst to her lips at his rambling of the invitation. "I'm so happy for them. I would love to see the wedding for two reasons—their happiness and maybe inspiration for the book."

"Okay, so nothing about the opportunity of spending time with me?"

She chuckled. "That's a given. Of course, that's the number one reason I'm excited." And it was absolutely true. She was falling for this man, and falling fast.

"You just made my day today and tomorrow. I'll be by to pick you up about five-thirty or a little earlier. The wedding is at six."

"I'll be ready. Is it dressy or casual?"

"Casual. It's on the beach and I wouldn't doubt if we are having grilled hot dogs or something similar."

"I can't wait. It sounds wonderful."

And it truly did. Especially because she would be going with Tucker.

* * *

After the news that Alice had told her in the kitchen,

WHAT A HEART'S DESIRE IS MADE OF

Lisa had been so happy for Riley and Sophie. However, her mind had gone to thoughts of Zane, who had basically worked silently beside her the last few days except when calling out instructions to the others. He was upset with her.

By the time they'd closed, she'd done something she rarely did and left the others to clean up while she went home. She'd needed time alone and now, here, sitting in the sand in the dark as the water rolled up several feet away from her, glistening in the moonlight, she struggled with her thoughts. She cared for Zane, and there was no doubt about it. No denying it.

But after all the things she'd gone through with her ex-husband, she couldn't let go of the fear that she could give her heart to someone and he would throw it into the garbage while he had an affair and then married the woman and had a child. She'd wanted children, and he'd denied them to her. She'd recently learned that Mason was going to be a father again.

She closed her eyes. At her age, Lisa knew after all the years he'd put his career ahead over having a family that now she was never going to have a family of her own. Part of that was not just her fifty-two years of age—actually very close to fifty-three, but because she couldn't bring herself to let someone get close enough to fall in love or marry again. At least, that had been her thoughts…and then she'd hired Zane. She'd been fighting the emotional trauma that had been building as he worked beside her and drew her toward him despite how she fought off thoughts about him. Then she'd gone on the boat ride with him…her heart hammered against her ribs just thinking about it.

What a mistake she'd made. She was in so much trouble now because nothing distracted her from thoughts of Zane. She crossed her arms on top of her knees and rested her chin on them. Her stomach churned as the reality of her situation filled her. She had to figure out how to shut down these feelings if she was to continue working with him. But how? She needed his talent and dedication in the busy kitchen.

"Lisa."

She jerked at the sound of her name coming from Zane. He stood a few feet behind her, highlighted in the moonlight. Her heart pounded. "What are you doing?"

"I thought you looked upset when you left, so after we finished cleaning up, I came to check on you. When you didn't answer your door, I thought I'd see if you were out here on the beach. And here you are."

He had come to check on her. It had been so long since a man had cared about her feelings.

"Can I join you?"

She wanted to say no but nodded before words came out. Oh yes, she was truly in so much trouble.

Zane took the three steps to reach her and then sank into the sand beside her. He had changed out of his chef suit like he often did and wore a pair of long cotton shorts and a green T-shirt with a fish over his heart. His heart… *Was he falling for her like she was falling for him, or was it just a wanting of her but not a real, true relationship?* She'd thought her ex had loved her and wanted her for forever, and the truth had knocked her hard. Knowing she was falling so hard for this man beside her terrified her, and she couldn't speak at the moment. Instead, she tore her gaze from him and stared back out to sea.

"What's wrong, Lisa?" Zane asked gently.

She had to tell him there was nothing she wanted between them. That she never could or would let herself love again…or admit it. She turned her head and faced him. "I need you…" She stopped midsentence as her gaze dropped to his lips. Her breath caught as longing for him swept over her like a huge, thundering wave from the ocean.

"And I need you," he said, joy in his words, and his lips turned to a smile. Then he leaned in and took her lips with his.

Lisa's eyes instantly closed as she leaned into him and his arms went around her. Emotions she'd never felt before in her life encased her. His kiss deepened and her hand that had gone to his heart felt his rate increase like hers. She loved this man. Loved him and there was no denying it. She'd been in the process of telling him she needed him to step back. To not try to get a relationship going between them. Stopping midsentence had her now in a deep ravine.

He broke the kiss and drew back, locking his gaze to hers. "I have been wanting you to say that for so long."

She swallowed hard as love and pain fought a battle inside her. She would never lose control of her life again and giving her love to someone meant they controlled her heart, the master of everything. "The kiss was good, but Zane, I didn't finish what I was saying. I was saying I need you to stop this. I don't want to fall for anyone ever again, and I won't. So I'm not trying to lead you on. I just need you as my helping chef."

He blinked and his expression was momentarily stunned.

She wanted to throw her arms around him and tell him she hadn't meant the words. But she didn't. It would be even more unfair to this man. The man she would not let herself trust. She would never do that again, and tonight was the night to stand her ground.

"You really mean that?"

"Yes. I'm sorry if I've given you the wrong impression. It was never my intention."

He placed his elbows on his knees and stared out to sea like she'd been doing when he'd arrived. "No need. It was me who pushed you. I'll go now and I'll not bother you again."

He stood and without another word, he walked back toward her home, where she was sure he'd parked his truck.

Her heart raged and every cell in her wanted to race to him, grab him, and tell him she hadn't meant it.

But she didn't.

CHAPTER NINETEEN

Tucker had picked up Maggie and now they were driving toward the gate of the camping grounds.

"Oh, it's beautiful." Maggie gasped, looking at the greenery wrapped around the poles and then the flowers draped over the campsite's sign hanging over the road.

It was beautiful but she was what he was looking at. Beautiful in so many, many ways. "Yes, very beautiful," he said as her gaze shifted to him and her eyes widened with realization that he was talking about her. He smiled. "Yes, *you* are beautiful."

"Thank you. But you know what I was talking about."

He drove through the gate and chuckled. "Yes, but

it's not as awesome as you are. Just letting you know." He was hoping he wasn't letting his mouth run too much, but he couldn't help it. Feelings for her were running out of control. He'd been alone and not attracted or having emotions this strong since losing his first love. *Love.* He shot his gaze to Maggie and his heart nearly exploded with what he felt for her.

He parked the truck beside the other vehicles. It looked as if they were the last to arrive. He could see them near the concession stand of the camp, all gathered around the wedding couple, exchanging hugs. He smiled. "I'm so happy for those two. Wait," he said, seeing her opening her door. "I'll get that, if you don't mind."

She smiled at him. "I don't mind. They do look happy. I can't wait to meet your brothers."

He climbed out, strode around the front of the truck and opened her door. He held his hand out for hers, and she slipped it into his as she slid from the truck seat. Tucker held back the desire to hug her and instead stepped back and then closed the door as she, too, stepped away to let him. He didn't let go of her hand as they headed across the gravel parking area to his family. Everyone turned to watch them approach, and he knew they were focused on the fact that he was holding her hand. It was something he never did, even when he'd taken those few ladies out when he'd tried dating.

Everyone began welcoming them.

Riley stepped forward. "We are so glad you got to come and bring Maggie. Maggie, I'm Riley, and you've met my bride Sophie. We are so glad you are joining in on our celebration."

"We certainly are." Sophie stepped up to give Maggie a hug. "I enjoyed our lunch with all the girls and am glad to see you again on my special day."

"I'm so glad Tucker asked me. I am excited for you, too, and a surprise wedding is just wonderful. Especially having it here where you fell in love…so very special."

Tucker squeezed her hand gently. "I'm glad to be here and glad she came with me. You two look overjoyed."

"Don't they?" his mother said, smiling. "Oh, Maggie, I want you to meet my husband, Seth. Seth, this is my new friend, Maggie Carson."

Tucker grinned as Seth leaned forward and gave Maggie a gentle hug.

"Very glad to meet you. I'm sorry for your loss and glad to see a sparkle in your eyes as you're making progress forward with your life. Been there and done that. God brought Alice into my life and this wonderful family unit. You're hanging out with a great guy." He smiled as he put his arm around Tucker's mom.

"I agree," Sophie said. "I'm about to enter this wonderful family and can't wait. But I can tell you, just being friends with all of you has been a dream come true for me. So, are y'all ready to go over the hill there, where our preacher and musician are waiting?"

"We're ready." Jackson took Nina's hand and placed it on his crooked arm. "Who is walking you down the aisle?"

Everyone echoed the question and Tucker did too.

Riley grinned as Sophie slipped her hand into the crook of his arm. "I am. So if y'all will go over the hill, you'll find the preacher, and the music will start. Then my dream comes true—I'll escort my beautiful soon-to-be wife down the path and join all of you for the ceremony."

Sophie was smiling at him, then smiled at everyone with eyes so full of joy that Tucker longed for Maggie to look at him with that kind of love glowing in her eyes.

Everyone fell into step behind Jackson and Nina, and he and Maggie took up the last position. He gave Maggie a warm smile and she returned it as they started walking. He glanced over his shoulder and shot the wedding couple a smile. Oh, how he wanted what they had. What he'd lost once and what he prayed he'd finally found once more.

* * *

The wedding area was beautiful, Maggie thought, as everyone gathered in the middle of small sand dunes, with the ocean visible. The music from the guitar began and the man playing it smiled at everyone, then looked past them. They all turned their heads and watched Riley and Sophie come over the slight hill and come to them, then take their place before the preacher, who smiled at them.

Maggie took everything in—the happiness of the

family's expressions as they watched the two say their vows, heard the love that was so very evident in Riley's and Sophie's voices and shining in their eyes. Maggie's gaze shifted to Tucker for a brief moment, taking in the joy for them on his face and in his soft golden eyes. Eyes she loved to look into, but she looked away quickly, not wanting him in this moment to catch her looking at him. Her heart pumped hard and fast as the preacher pronounced them husband and wife. Everyone cheered and clapped as they wrapped their arms around each other and kissed. Maggie remembered that moment when she and Mark had kissed as husband and wife for the first time. Her heart ached for that moment at the same time it swelled with happiness for these two.

Grinning joyously, the two held hands and walked past everyone, heading back the way they'd come.

"Please join us for a celebration," Riley said, looking back at them all with a grin. "It's time to celebrate our joy. Time to celebrate me being the happiest man in the world."

"Ha!" Dallas yelped. "You can join me, but you can't beat me." He smiled down at Lorna, then kissed her gently on her smiling lips.

"I'm in the group too," Jackson declared as he kissed Nina's waiting lips.

Seth chuckled and hugged Alice closer to his side. "I'm glad to be in that group also." He kissed her forehead, and Alice smiled a beautiful smile.

Maggie remembered those feelings.

"Well then," Riley said, grinning widely. "I'm just glad to finally be in the McIntyre clan of happiness."

Everyone followed the newlyweds into the big tent Maggie had noticed earlier. It had a concrete floor and a large enough table set up for all of them to sit and enjoy dinner. Soft music played over speakers, and a table on the side with a white tablecloth and silver warming containers had something in them that smelled delicious. Small lights glistened from the ceiling and beautiful vases of red roses were everywhere. Even on the table where a three-tier white wedding cake sat, with a small figure of two newlyweds embracing on the top. It was all beautiful.

Tucker still held her hand and she leaned into his arm, getting closer to his ear as she whispered, "It's so charming." He turned his face to hers and now just a thin space separated them. Her gaze locked with his, and her heart went crazy.

"I agree. Simple but great," he said softly, his gaze digging deep. "I'm…glad you came with me."

"I am too." And she was. "I just have to move slow."

"I understand. We'll move as slow as you need to move."

CHAPTER TWENTY

Zane's heart stung as he stared off the deck of his home into the dark night. Ever since the conversation he and Lisa had after he'd kissed her two weeks ago, he'd been struggling to stand there at work beside her and keep his love for her behind closed doors. She'd made her point clear and put him in his place, and he knew it was her right as his boss.

He'd let his feelings free and felt her kiss him back when he'd jumped in there and kissed her. He'd misunderstood what she'd said to him and fulfilled what he'd been wanting to do for so long by immediately kissing her and loving every second of it. Then to have her tell him she didn't want this attraction to go any further—she wanted it gone and for them to only work together—now he couldn't get his heart and head back on track of just being her kitchen helper.

The whole last two weeks since that night on the beach with her had been like this. He knew he had to change something. In his heart, he felt she had similar feelings, if that kiss was any sign, but she was intent on pushing him from her emotional and physical life. Of reminding him that he was just her assistant. He knew now, after two weeks of trying, that he couldn't continue like this, with these overwhelming feelings for her.

His phone rang and he looked at his watch, shocked that his phone would be ringing at eleven-thirty at night. He was even more shocked and alarmed that it was a call from his nephew, whom he hadn't heard from much ever since the younger man had gotten married and now focused his life on his wife and new baby.

He immediately answered the call, it being this late set alarms ringing. "Dave, is something wrong?"

"I…need you." His only nephew's ragged, odd-sounding voice rang in Zane's ears. His brother Nick had raised Dave after his mother died at birth and then

Nick died a few years ago leaving him and Dave as the only family members. Dave had taken it hard and Zane had tried to be there for him as much as possible.

Now, he gripped the phone. "What's wrong?"

"H...hospital in College Station...need you." And the phone went dead.

Zane's heart pounded as he redialed the number, but it just rang and rang; no one answered.

Zane was already in the house and headed into his room. Within minutes, he had a small suitcase packed, lights out and the house locked up as he climbed into his truck and headed off Star Gazer Island. He had to get to Dave and his wife and baby. He had to get there fast because he knew something terrible had happened. He'd heard it in Dave's voice.

He was already across the bridge before he thought about work. It was too late to call Lisa, so he would call in the morning.

He thought about trying to fly but this late there would be no flights and it was only about five hours away, so he pressed the gas pedal and focused on shortening the drive as much as possible.

Dave hadn't sounded good. *Had something happened to his wife or had something happened to both of them? And their baby—was he okay?* Questions swirled through his head and his fingers gripped the steering wheel tighter and tighter. He had to fight not to press harder on the gas pedal. He had to get there, and he was already taking a risk by how fast he was going. Getting there was the most important point. His whole life had been about getting there. About overcoming and making something of his life and he'd done that despite everything. But when he'd finally thought he'd found love and a new start, it wasn't happening. Lisa didn't want him. And now worry about the only people in the world he truly, deeply cared about and were all he had left, had him panicking.

He felt desperate as he sped the hours toward them.

* * *

Alice was so happy at home with Seth and also at work. She loved the inn and seeing the smiling faces of her customers as they came in and out, enjoying their vacation. Enjoying their food. They absolutely loved the food. She realized as she finished checking someone out that she hadn't seen Lisa all morning, so she headed into the kitchen area to see how things were going. Lisa always came out in between getting things set up and before she started cooking, so her absence this morning was off a bit.

The moment Alice entered the kitchen, she stopped. Everyone was working hard, especially Lisa over at her grill area. She was working the whole grill as she used to do, and Zane was not around. Alice looked toward the freezer, where he often was coming out with trays of meat or something they needed but there was no sign of the amazing chef.

She strode across the room to Lisa. "Is everything okay? You look like you are doing all this on your own."

Lisa glanced at her. "Sorry, I didn't have time to come out and tell you. Zane called a few moments ago. He's in College Station, where his only close relative lives. His nephew and his wife…they were both killed in a home fire last night. His nephew was able to call him before he died at the hospital and asked him to come. Zane was upset when he called me. The baby made it, after his daddy got him out and into a neighbor's arms before he turned and went back in after his wife. It's horrible, Alice. So horrible, but thankfully the baby is in the hospital getting treated for smoke inhalation, and Zane is by his side."

Shock and sadness rolled over Alice. It was evident by the look in Lisa's eyes and the sound of her wavering voice that Lisa felt the same. "This is terrible. I feel so sorry for him and the baby…and the loss of his mother and dad. Can I help you? Do you need to sit down, take a break?"

Lisa was concentrating on the food, and she shook her head. "I need this right now. Need something to keep me busy. I am so broken-hearted for Zane and this poor baby. But, working will keep me going until he calls again."

Alice knew her friend and knew that working was her way to keep her world rotating through the hard hits of life. She placed a hand on her arm. "Okay, I'll be checking in if you need me. I'll be praying the baby comes out good. I'm so sorry for Zane but glad he's there to stand by that baby's side."

Lisa glanced at her and nodded but couldn't speak;

it was evident by the strain in her eyes. Alice gently squeezed her arm then headed out of the kitchen, giving her dear friend the space she needed.

Had her friend acknowledged that she loved Zane?

Hopefully things would work out. Alice pulled her phone from her pocket and called Seth. He and Zane had become friends after Zane bought a house down the street from them. He loved the ocean view, the pier, and fishing just like Seth did, so she called him with the news.

"That's terrible," Seth said, having paused what he was working on at the house he was remodeling. "He hasn't called me, but if he needs something looked out for at his house, I'm sure he will call so I'm not going to call him today. But tomorrow I'll check in on him if I don't hear from him."

"That sounds good. He's watching over a baby. I don't know how old but I think he's not even a year old yet."

"Yeah, he mentioned that they were going to come down and visit later this summer after the baby was a few months older. If I remember right, he might be seven months or maybe when they were coming, he would be seven months."

Alice thought of her sweet grandbaby she'd inherited when Dallas and Lorna married. Little Landon had been born after Dallas had found Lorna on the beach and he'd carried her to the inn to have the baby. Thank goodness her little Landon now had his mom and Dallas to love him, and all of their family now claimed him as theirs. She wondered whether this little boy Zane now stood beside and watched over had anyone else or whether Zane was now his guardian.

"It just hit me," she said into the phone, glad she'd asked one of her helpers to take over the front desk and she'd come out into the flower garden area. "Do you think Zane will be the baby's guardian now? I mean, for life, not just in the hospital?"

Her husband didn't say anything at first, and she was sure the same thoughts she was thinking were flowing through his head too. "He might be. As far as I know, his nephew, his wife, and the baby were all the family Zane and they had."

She sighed. "This could completely change his life."

"With just the short friendship I've had with Zane,

I can tell you he'll step up. So, Alice, just a warning—Lisa may lose her chef."

"Yes, that's what I was thinking too. Okay, I'll let you get back to work. I just wanted you to know what was going on, and I needed to hear your voice."

"I love you, Alice and am so thankful for you. For this baby, the one really good thought about all this sadness going on in his life and in Zane's life is that at least the child has him. Zane will do whatever the child needs."

They hung up, and she was certain that Seth was right. Whatever the child needed Zane would do it…even if that meant giving up his job, his home, and moving to wherever this child needed to be if he was the one who would be raising him.

What would Lisa think about that? How bad would her friend be hurt?

Of course, there were many other things that could happen. But right now, in her heart, this was the one that rang loudest.

CHAPTER TWENTY-ONE

Maggie spent much of the week after Sophie and Riley's romantic wedding hanging out with Tucker as he took her to many beautiful spots on the ranch and also took her to watch a day of the ranchhands working the cattle, giving them shots and checking their overall health. It was a wonderful week and she'd loved spending the time with Tucker.

Today, as she sat at her kitchen table, drinking her morning coffee and staring at the story coming alive on her computer, she wasn't really paying attention to what she was reading. Her thoughts were on Tucker and how being with him had lifted her spirits so much. Gave her a vision of a new life. A new love…something she'd never, ever envisioned she would want. The words "new love" rang repeatedly through her head. *Had she really fallen in love so quickly since meeting Tucker?*

Could it be possible?

She had fallen for Mark quickly and had never ever felt this way but for him…and now Tucker. Her mind whirling, she stood up. There was no writing getting done today, and she needed groceries. She grabbed her purse and headed to her car. Just the steps forward put her mind on something more, at least for a few minutes, as she got in and headed toward Star Gazer Island. It didn't take too long to travel down the back road and then start across the small bridge, small compared to the one farther down that took you up and over to Corpus Christi and that ships could cross beneath. This was a small island and only small boats crossed under this bridge, so the up and down was quick and easy.

Still, she loved it. She was behind a convertible with its top down and the woman's hair blew in the wind. Instantly, Maggie wished she had a convertible. She had wanted one earlier in her marriage, but they lived in a busy area and Mark had worried about her and talked her out of it. But as she followed this car, the want slammed over her again, as did the desire to live here.

Her pulse jumped at the thought and began rushing as she drove off the bridge onto the road. The beautiful island was actually connected on the other end to the mainland, so many might not consider it an island. But to those who had originally named it, they'd been as she was, and saw it as a beautiful island.

Instead of going to the grocery store, she passed it by, she was so caught up in her thoughts. She drove to where roads split off from the main road and houses could be seen that had backyards that connected to the water. She turned onto the road, then slowed down, admiring the houses—some small cabin types and some large two- and three-story homes. They all drew her, but the small ones were where her eyes were most drawn.

The road curved, following the way the island was shaped. She knew this particular road probably would end somewhere, but she was officially exploring now. She followed the curve and instantly pressed the brake when a small teal-toned bungalow came into view and a For Sale sign stood in the yard.

Without another thought, she pulled into the driveway. The cottage was so beautiful, with the teal color of the water making it even more attractive. There were no cars in the drive and she was suddenly driven to find out more as her gaze went to the sign. She pulled her phone from her purse. Was she really doing this?

Absolutely.

She dialed the number on the sign. She was immediately talking to a real-estate saleswoman, who said she was not too far away and would be there in just a few minutes to show her around. Maggie disconnected the call and sat there, staring at the house. *Again, was she really doing this?*

She climbed out and walked beneath the carport that was connected to the house, through the opening, and into the backyard. Her heart paused as she gasped at the beauty of the small green yard with a wooden fence line on both sides giving privacy and then a concrete strip along the water with a boat dock and a deck for relaxing on. No beach at this part of the island but a gorgeous view of the ocean. For those moments, she lost herself staring out across the water glistening, with the sunlight shining down upon it.

"I see you found the beautiful view."

She spun to find a short, pretty woman who looked to be about forty, and she was smiling. Maggie smiled too. "It's wonderful. Are you here to show the house to me?"

The lady held her hand out and crossed to her. "I'm Pam Hughes and I can't wait to show you this house. It actually just went on the market this morning. That sign hasn't been up more than an hour, so you're the first person to see it. Follow me. We'll enter from this lovely back porch entrance. I'm sure you can figure out at a glance that the house won't last long on the market."

The moment she'd seen the sign, Maggie had assumed it wouldn't last long, so her assumption was right. Pam pushed the glass door open and let her step in first. The living room mingling with the kitchen on the far side welcomed her, and though there was no furniture in it, she saw a vision of what she would put inside. She turned back toward the glass windows and door just as Pam clicked the lights on. Not that they were needed; even though the porch had a cover on it, cutting some of the sunlight from the room, the brightness was still great.

Her heart hammering, she walked over to the kitchen, taking in the pretty counters and the soft white cabinets and the large eating and entertaining bar that separated the kitchen from the living room. It was not a huge house, but it was made for a small private life or entertaining small to midsized groups.

She didn't need to see more. Oh, she would, but she knew she wanted it. "How much? And are there any problems?"

Pam smiled and the numbers came instantly. It had been remodeled and was in tip-top shape and it wasn't cheap, but Maggie had already known it wouldn't be because it was too perfect. The lovely area it was in had to be so popular that would make the price head up the hill at high speed. She breathed in a deep breath. With her career and the sale of her and Mark's house, plus all he'd done with savings and death insurance, she could do this.

She was ready to do this, needed to do this. "I'll take it."

Pam's eyes widened. "You will? I mean, it's a great buy. I just wasn't expecting you to take it so quickly."

Maggie placed a hand on her hip. "It's beautiful, and I have no doubt the moment people get a whiff that it's for sale, it won't last long. I'm single and it's the perfect size for me. The fact is…I need a change."

A huge smile waved across the Realtor's face. "Then if you'd like to follow me to my office, we'll get the paperwork started."

"Perfect. Lead the way." Excitement vibrated through Maggie. She needed to find a way to move forward, and this was her step. Her thoughts went to what was building between her and Tucker, but she could not let that move too fast. This was another reason this was a good move. She needed a bit of space between them; she needed to know that she'd made a good decision about moving her life forward first. Her mind would be clear then, about knowing whether she really had space in her heart for another love. Others did— Tucker's mother did and her love for her first husband had been like Maggie's for Mark. As she thought of Mark, Tucker's gentle smile filled her vision.

WHAT A HEART'S DESIRE IS MADE OF

She pulled into the car space next to the real-estate office. Tucker's smile in her thoughts gave her more assurance that she was making the right move. If they were to find out whether what they were feeling was real, then her being here was the perfect move…if it fell apart, she felt as though they'd survive because they'd both survived the loss of their first loves. Knowing this, she knew they could survive anything.

She got out of the car and headed into the real-estate office as Tucker's handsome face and intense eyes filled her thoughts even more. It hit her hard then: *could she really get over it if he walked away?*

* * *

"So where are we going?" Tucker glanced over at Maggie, who looked very excited in the truck's seat as she told him which road to turn onto. She'd called and asked him whether he had time to let her show him something when he got off work, and of course he did. He'd take time off to spend every moment he had with her.

"You'll see in just a few more short moments.

Follow this road around that curve up there." He did as she said, and then she placed her hand on his arm. "Pull in there." She pointed at the driveway of the cute ocean-toned cottage.

He then parked the truck and looked at her. "Who lives here?"

She beamed, with a warm smile and sparkling eyes. "Soon, I will. I'm buying it. Paperwork began today."

His jaw dropped open and then he gave a chuckle of joy. "Wow, that's great. Wow, you acted fast. Or have you been planning this for a while?"

"Fast. I saw it this morning and knew this was where I was going to start over. What do you think?"

His heart pounded. He knew they couldn't move too fast, but this solved the problem of her moving back home. She was going to be here, close to the ranch and him. "I like it. Love it, actually."

"Then come on in and let me show it to you."

They climbed from the truck, then he followed her through the carport to the back, where the ocean view greeted them. She stopped on the porch, but Tucker strode out to the center of the grass and looked at the ocean glistening with a great view. He turned back to look at Maggie standing with her arms crossed and an enticing, beautiful smile on her lips.

Hope slammed into him. "You're really buying this?"

"Yes. The papers are processing as we speak. I found it this morning and the Realtor came right over and showed it to me. I grabbed it immediately. I knew it was right. Even if you realize along the way as we date and explore our feelings for each other that I'm not the woman you can love, I know we can still make it living in the same town."

Her words slammed into him like a sledgehammer. He deleted the space between them with just a few steps and placed his hands on her shoulders, forcing himself not to pull her against him. "I can promise you, from my viewpoint, that will never happen. Maggie, I want to bow to my knee right now and ask you to marry me, but I know that's too soon for you. I totally understand. But I'm here and trying to prepare myself for if you decide that I'm not the man to step into the footprints that Mark left on your heart. I understand if that's what you decide. I'm rooting for you, and I'll take whatever your heart decides."

"Tucker—"

Tears suddenly streamed down her face, and he wanted to kiss them away as his heart pounded. Gently, he cupped her face and let his thumbs smooth the wetness from her cheeks. "Please don't cry."

"I'm struggling. Trying so hard not to just say 'Yes, please marry me.' I can't let myself jump into something, even as wonderful as it sounds to me. Even as comforting and full of promise that it gives me."

Her words filled him with hope, not distress. "I'm here for you and truly understand everything you are feeling. We will make this trip together. Can I kiss you?"

Her hands went to his waist and then slid around him. "Please. Now, let this adventure to heart healing proceed. It feels right. So right. And, Tucker, just so you know, I can't see Mark smiling with happiness, but I feel it in my soul that he's happy we found each other."

Deep, hard emotion waved over him. "Then he knows I'll always have your heart, your well-being, and your happiness as my main goal as we travel toward a life together. I value you and your love so much." Unable to stop himself, he lowered his lips to hers. His hands slid into her hair as he cherished the feel of her and the goodness of her as she kissed him back. His heart swelled as he felt the smiles of his Darla and her Mark looking down on them.

Life had terribly hard sorrows to bear but love could help heal the pain when hearts were allowed to open to new possibilities.

He pulled his lips away just enough to peer into her eyes. "I love you and always will, Maggie."

Her eyes glistened. "And I feel the same for you. I never thought I'd say these words again, but Tucker…I love you so very much and am so thankful you feel the same for me." She slipped her hand around his neck and pulled his lips back to hers.

He went gratefully, happily, and excitedly. This love story was theirs. He wanted to turn the pages rapidly but would instead cherish each moment they had together.

And he prayed it was many.

EPILOGUE

The afternoon sun gleamed down on the thick sand as Alice and Lisa crossed it, heading to the water and a walk along the shoreline. Smiles filled every nook of her as she told Lisa of all the wonderful things going on in her life. The coming of Nina and Jackson's baby birth progressed slowly but her grandbaby's arrival drew closer with every passing day. As did Dallas and Lorna's newly announced baby, due just after Christmas, while Nina and Jackson's baby was due just before Christmas. December was going to be so special this year. The thought of little sweet Landon having a baby brother or sister brought a bigger smile to her face. She and Seth were ready for as many grandchildren as they were given by her kids. She even had a feeling that the newly wed Riley and Sophie were also working at becoming parents.

Her excitement was just about her kids being parents, but everyone was thrilled that Tucker and Maggie were now officially dating seriously. It was prayers answered and delightful to watch. Those two had lost so much but were now seeing, like she did, that love never dies but a heart can make more room for new love. She was so very grateful for that because she'd loved her William with all her heart and had been startled by her love for Seth. She'd fallen in love with the special, caring man and been lucky to have found it again. She glanced at Lisa and so hoped she would move forward from the dark lines in her past and find true love and happiness.

They reached packed, damp sand and immediately started their stroll that she'd talked Lisa into taking with her. It was obvious to everyone that Lisa needed to get outside for a bit and Alice wanted to be filled in on what was going on with Lisa and Zane. She might tell Lisa about how excited she was about grandkids and her own happiness in life, but Lisa didn't talk as openly about what was going on with her. But Alice knew after a week of Zane being gone that Lisa was battling emotions that needed to be exposed.

"Enough about my family. It's time for you to talk, my sweet friend." Alice reached out to take hold of Lisa's forearm and stopped walking. "Please look at me." Lisa stopped walking too, sadness filling her eyes. "I know Zane lost his only close family member and his wife, and he had to go and is now there for the baby. Seth has talked with him a couple of times and we know he's trying to figure out everything about the baby's future since he is now his guardian." The expression on Lisa's face startled her. "Did you not know that?"

"No. He called me once that first morning to tell me he wouldn't be in for work and told me what had happened. He called again, just the other day, with a quick call telling me I would have to find someone to take his job because he wasn't sure he'd be back. He said nothing about being a guardian of the baby. Why didn't he tell me any of this?"

Alice was so shocked by this knowledge that she just stared at her friend and the anguish in her eyes. "Did something happen between you two?"

Lisa spun to face the water and wrapped her arms tightly about her waist. "He kissed me."

Happiness blasted through Alice. She jumped in front of her dear friend, smiling at her with joy. "And you are sad about that? I've thought he was attracted to you from the beginning." She stopped smiling. "Why are you so sad about this? You look like you're going to cry."

"No, I'm not going to cry. I was in the middle of telling him there would never be anything between us when he did it. When he *kissed* me. He misunderstood what I was saying because I hesitated. But afterwards...I finished my words and told him our relationship would never be more than coworkers. He left and we managed to work the next couple of weeks together but with much strain between us. Then he got the call about his nephew. Now, I can't stop thinking that he might never come back."

Heart pounding, Alice fought off the need to put her arms around her friend. "He will be back. I just know he will. And if what Seth said about the little boy becoming Zane's is true, then he won't be alone and maybe he'll need some help."

Lisa's expression tightened. "It wouldn't be me he asked for help. You and I both know that I know very little about children."

"Look, my dear friend, you need to get a grip. You've lived through a lot of bad stuff and decided you didn't deserve anything else because you're afraid of hoping and loving again. You have to let that go. Please let it go, and let good things happen in your personal life. Don't shut someone out, especially if he shows up and needs you."

Lisa looked down at the moist sand, and Alice was certain she was blinking away tears trying to form in her eyes. Finally, she looked up. "I love you, good friend, and am so happy things have worked out so well for you. But I can't make that promise. I can just hope…and pray that Zane and this sweet baby make it okay. I'm sure Zane will be wonderful with the child. He learns quickly and he smiles a lot. So like you with your grandchildren now, he'll laugh a lot more with the joy the baby will bring into his life." She leaned forward and wrapped her arms around Alice. "Thanks for your concern but I'll be fine. I always am. Now, I have a kitchen to get back to." She let go and headed back toward the inn and the kitchen.

Alice didn't move. She watched her dear friend leave and hoped with all of her heart that something in her broken heart and mind would change. Alice had so much in her life to look forward to. Grandchildren and just dinner with the man she loved with all her heart. But now, Alice hoped and prayed that despite Lisa's negative outlook that her heart would open up and love would find her again, just like it had for Alice.

Her phone rang and she pulled it out of her pocket.

Seth's handsome face looked at her from the screen and she smiled as she pressed the Accept button. "I'm so glad you called," she said, meaning it so deeply.

"I'm so glad you answered. I have a boat ready to take you out for a ride and a meal at sunset. What do you think?"

Alice closed her eyes and let her heart wrap gratefully around his words. "I so need that ride. I'll be there soon. I love you, Seth." And she meant it with all her heart.

"I love you, too, and will be here when you arrive. You are everything my heart has ever desired and more, my love."

"And you are the same for me."

As she headed toward the inn, the place where she'd met both loves of her life, she smiled. If it was meant to be between Lisa and Zane, meeting each other here at this Star Gazer Inn like they did said it all…never give up on love. When the time is right, love will be there. It had been for her and she would believe with all of her heart that it would be there for her dear friend.

WHAT A HEART'S DESIRE IS MADE OF

Her smile grew as she thought of Seth and knew his arms would soon wrap around her as she climbed onto the boat with him. She'd opened her heart again and was so thankful she'd done so. When the time was right she prayed Lisa would do the same.

Dear Readers—don't miss Lisa and Zane's heartfelt love story, *What True Love Is Made Of*.
Preorder today!

WHAT TRUE LOVE IS MADE OF
Star Gazer Inn of Corpus Christi Bay, book Five

Life on Star Gazer Island and the McIntyre Ranch near Corpus Christi Texas is progressing wonderfully for Alice since finding love again and watching her sons do the same.

And now babies are on the way! Let the fun began.

But her friend Lisa hasn't been so lucky, and as happy

as Alice is her heart is hurting for Lisa. But Alice is rooting for the attraction she sees between Lisa and her assistant chef, Zane.

After her horrible divorce Lisa Blair has found satisfaction being the chef at Star Gazer Inn and is delighted about everyone's newfound love. However, she had no plan about falling in love again herself, then she hired chef, Zane Tyson...and now life has become complicated. Now she's in trouble, especially after he's called out on a family emergency and might not ever return.

Zane's heart is broken after being pushed away by Lisa, the only woman he's ever loved. Now after a horrible fire, his nephew and his young wife are dead and Zane is called to their baby's side. A single man all of his life, he is now the baby's guardian and not sure how to handle it.

Now what? He's going to need help so he returns to Star

WHAT A HEART'S DESIRE IS MADE OF

Gazer Island where he knows there will be help from his friends…and maybe Alice.

Also, newly in love Tucker McIntyre and Maggie Carson are moving forward in their romance, taking it slow but steady as everyone is rooting for them.

And then all of Tucker's brothers and their wonderful wives are expecting babies…hopefully a wedding, and a baby will be in store for him and Maggie.

Don't miss this trip to Star Gazer Island…romance surrounds everyone!

More Books by Debra Clopton

Star Gazer Inn of Corpus Christi Bay
What New Beginnings are Made of (Book 1)
What Dreams are Made of (Book 2)
What Hopes are Made of (Book 3)
What a Heart's Desire is Made of (Book 4)
What True Love is Made of (Book 5)

Sunset Bay Romance
Longing for Forever (Book 1)
Longing for a Hero (Book 2)
Longing for Love (Book 3)
Longing for Ever After (Book 4)
Longing for You (Book 5)
Longing for Us (Book 6)

Texas Brides & Bachelors
Heart of a Cowboy (Book 1)
Trust of a Cowboy (Book 2)
True Love of a Cowboy (Book 3)

New Horizon Ranch Series
Her Texas Cowboy: Cliff (Book 1)
Rescued by Her Cowboy: Rafe (Book 2)
Protected by Her Cowboy: Chase (Book 3)
Loving Her Best Friend Cowboy: Ty (Book 4)
Family for a Cowboy: Dalton (Book 5)
The Mission of Her Cowboy: Treb (Book 6)
Maddie's Secret Baby (Book 7)
This Cowgirl Loves This Cowboy: Austin (Book 8)

Turner Creek Ranch Series
Treasure Me, Cowboy (Book 1)
Rescue Me, Cowboy (Book 2)
Complete Me, Cowboy (Book 3)
Sweet Talk Me, Cowboy (Book 4)

Cowboys of Ransom Creek
Her Cowboy Hero (Book 1)
The Cowboy's Bride for Hire (Book 2)
Cooper: Charmed by the Cowboy (Book 3)
Shane: The Cowboy's Junk-Store Princess (Book 4)
Vance: Her Second-Chance Cowboy (Book 5)
Drake: The Cowboy and Maisy Love (Book 6)
Brice: Not Quite Looking for a Family (Book 7)

Texas Matchmaker Series
Dream With Me, Cowboy (Book 1)
Be My Love, Cowboy (Book 2)
This Heart's Yours, Cowboy (Book 3)
Hold Me, Cowboy (Book 4)
Be Mine, Cowboy (Book 5)
Operation: Married by Christmas (Book 6)
Cherish Me, Cowboy (Book 7)
Surprise Me, Cowboy (Book 8)
Serenade Me, Cowboy (Book 9)
Return To Me, Cowboy (Book 10)
Love Me, Cowboy (Book 11)
Ride With Me, Cowboy (Book 12)
Dance With Me, Cowboy (Book 13)

Windswept Bay Series
From This Moment On (Book 1)
Somewhere With You (Book 2)
With This Kiss (Book 3)
Forever and For Always (Book 4)
Holding Out For Love (Book 5)
With This Ring (Book 6)
With This Promise (Book 7)
With This Pledge (Book 8)
With This Wish (Book 9)
With This Forever (Book 10)
With This Vow (Book 11)

About the Author

Bestselling author Debra Clopton has sold over 2.5 million books. Her book OPERATION: MARRIED BY CHRISTMAS has been optioned for an ABC Family Movie. Debra is known for her contemporary, western romances, Texas cowboys and feisty heroines. Sweet romance and humor are always intertwined to make readers smile. A sixth generation Texan she lives with her husband on a ranch deep in the heart of Texas. She loves being contacted by readers.

Visit Debra's website at www.debraclopton.com

Sign up for Debra's newsletter at
www.debraclopton.com/contest/

Check out her Facebook at
www.facebook.com/debra.clopton.5

Follow her on Twitter at @debraclopton

Contact her at debraclopton@ymail.com

If you enjoyed reading *What a Heart's Desire is Made of*, I would appreciate it if you would help others enjoy this book, too.

Recommend it. Please help other readers find this book by recommending it to friends, reader's groups and discussion boards.

Review it. Please tell other readers why you liked this book by reviewing it on the retail site you purchased it from or Goodreads. If you do write a review, please send an email to debraclopton@ymail.com so I can thank you with a personal email. Or visit me at: www.debraclopton.com.

Made in the USA
Monee, IL
29 August 2021